HUCKERMAN'S NOON

The hell-raising bunch raided and torched the high plains homestead, left widower Tom Huckerman for dead and abducted his twelve-year-old daughter. But Huckerman was a man of stubborn resolve, with a past that boded a haunted future for those who crossed him. His long-buried secret from way back travelled easy — packed in the shape of twin Colts all set to blaze whenever he had a mind, and wherever the shadows of the hell-raisers dared to walk.

Books by Luther Chance
in the Linford Western Library:

GUN RAGE

LUTHER CHANCE

HUCKERMAN'S NOON

Complete and Unabridged

LINFORD
Leicester

First published in Great Britain in 1999 by
Robert Hale Limited
London

First Linford Edition
published 2000
by arrangement with
Robert Hale Limited
London

British Library CIP Data

Chance, Luther
Huckerman's noon.—Large print ed.—
Linford western library
1. Western stories
2. Large type books
I. Title
823.9'14 [F]

ISBN 0–7089–5789–7

Published by
F. A. Thorpe (Publishing)
Anstey, Leicestershire

Set by Words & Graphics Ltd.
Anstey, Leicestershire
Printed and bound in Great Britain by
T. J. International Ltd., Padstow, Cornwall

This book is printed on acid-free paper

This for J.F.P.
with every good wish

1

Ten miles out of Trulso, on a day when the land held its breath and the sun blazed high in a straight blue sky, six men pillaged and burned to the dirt the Huckerman homestead.

They took whatever worth the taking from that lean life property, scattered the hogs from their rough fenced pens, the hens from their roosts, the dogs from their shack, and left for dead in a pool of blood the man whose home the spread had once been.

It was only as an afterthought that they rounded up Tom Huckerman's twelve-year-old daughter, Holly, trussed her tight to a spare mount and rode out heading due west, deep into the Broken Neck mountains.

And that, at a time in a wilderness territory where life and loss stood no better than the dust at a man's feet, and came and went twice as cheap, might have been the last anybody heard of the scratch-farming, quiet-eyed widower and his yellow-haired daughter and their home on the high plain out of Trulso.

It might, as history would have written it, been just cold ash on a long wind.

But Tom Huckerman did not die in his spilled blood on that day and his daughter did not close her eyes ever again without the thought that some-where out there, come spring, come summer, the chasing chill of fall, the snowswept winter, her pa would be following, waiting on his chance to take her back to where she belonged.

That was the dream that built the legend of one man's devotion to a timeless search.

★   ★   ★

'Damn it, Tom Huckerman, if yuh ain't just the most mule-headed man I ever clapped eyes on! And that's puttin' it straight as I know how, 'spite of sympathizin' with yuh. Hell, man, ain't it never occurred to yuh . . . ' Sheriff Ed Woods thumped a thick, heavy fist on his desk, rattled an empty tin mug, stared at the man facing him, then slumped back in his chair with a sigh. 'No, it ain't,' he groaned, 'so I'm just wastin' good breath.'

'That you most certainly are,' said the man, his gaze narrowing as he crossed the office to the dust-smeared window overlooking the sparse main street of the town of Trulso. 'There ain't no arguin' to be done here, Ed, and yuh know better than to try.' He half-turned. 'I'm pullin' out at noon.'

'Yeah, yeah, so yuh keep tellin' me,' sighed the sheriff, wiping a hand over his sticky face. 'Yuh been tellin' me just that for the past hour — and I ain't stoppin' yuh. 'Course I ain't. No man would. Ever a fella had reason to do what yuh plannin', you got it. Can't argue that. But yuh gotta think

3

this through, Tom.'

'Yuh think I haven't?' croaked the man, his stare flat on the sun-hazed street. 'That's all I been doin' this past month holed-up there in the roomin'-house, waitin' on this darned body of mine mendin' fit to move. Wakin' on the thought, sleepin' on it, seein' it all the time between. Every last detail. Hearin' every last sound. I'm all through with thinkin', Ed.'

'Sure yuh are,' soothed Ed, steepling his fingers at his chin. 'I can understand that, but it's them four weeks that troubles me. A whole month, Tom, and we ain't a spit closer to knowin' what happened to them scum after they left your place than the day they torched it. Not a lick. Damn it, I've had a dozen men and more, m'self along of 'em, scourin' them hills 'til it seems like there ain't a rock, a scrap of brush, we ain't turned over. I know every creek, darn near every crack and drift for thirty sweat-sodden miles in any direction — could even get to recognizin' the dirt! — and there ain't nothin', not a thing. It's like them sonsofbitches just vanished clean off this earth. And that's a fact.'

'But they're out there,' murmured the man. 'And Holly along of 'em.'

Sheriff Woods sighed again and came slowly, carefully to his feet behind the desk. 'Yeah, well, mebbe she is at that,' he said, running a finger over the coffee-stained desk.

'No mebbe about it, Ed,' snapped the man. 'She *is*. I know it.'

'Yuh gotta hold to that, sure yuh have, just like we all do, every man and woman hereabouts, but truth is — '

The man turned quickly from the window. 'What truth, Ed?' he hissed. 'Whose truth? What yuh sayin' there? Yuh sayin' as how — '

'Now hold on. Steady up,' calmed Ed, raising an arm. 'I ain't sayin' nothin' that steps outa my experience, but when yuh wearin' this badge yuh see things as they are, not as yuh want 'em to be. That way yuh don't get to bein' disappointed none and yuh save on the grievin'. And yuh stay alive!' He paused to stare deep into the man's eyes. 'Yuh gotta face it, Tom, chances are them vermin weren't for wastin' too much time on a twelve year old. Way I see it, they had only one good reason for takin' her: to sell her.'

The man stiffened, a nerve twitching in his cheek.

'Puttin' it plain, gal that age, pretty with it and growin' to be a good-lookin' young woman, would fetch a snappy price. Sioux, Apache, roughneck drifters, some two-bit saloon back of nowhere, they'd all be willin' buyers. Straight deal, no questions asked.' Sheriff Woods ran a hand over his face again. 'Fact, Tom,' he grunted, 'and yuh'd best shape to it.'

'The hell I will!'

'And *if* I'm right and *if* she's some place still breathin', yuh got about as much chance of findin' her and squarin' with them rats who took her as yuh have of shovellin' them hills out there into a hole! Hell, we don't even know who them fellas were! Never seen 'em, so who we lookin' for, f'Crissake? Best yuh can do, Tom, is let me get word round the territory for folk to keep their eyes skinned and the law to stay lookin'. T'ain't to say yuh won't get lucky, and who knows — '

'That your idea of the truth, Ed?' said the man, suddenly composed and easy again. 'That it, or some version of it?'

'Now I ain't sayin' — ' began Ed.

'Let me tell yuh the truth way I see it.' The man moved closer to the desk. 'Truth is, ten years back, when May died like she did in that home we built with our own hands and sweat and left me to raise Holly, still a wet-butted two year old, weren't a deal of me worth the botherin'. Didn't look to be much of a future from there on. But we made it, Ed, like hell we did! Scorched summers, frozen winters, sometimes darn near little enough to eat, stock that never got no fatter than a beanpole . . . We had 'em all, and still lived.'

7

'I know all that, Tom,' gestured Ed, 'and there ain't a body this side of the Broken Necks wouldn't take their hat off to yuh for what yuh done. Not a man. But that don't change — '

'Day them scumbag rattlers torched my place and took Holly, they finished things for good. No home, no stock, m'self whipped clean outa my senses, and *no daughter*.' The man paused, his gaze tight as ice. 'Last thing I promised May when she lay dyin' out there was how I'd look to Holly no matter what. She'd grow good and decent, just like her ma planned for her. Put my word on it, and I ain't for breakin' it.' He settled his hands on the desk and leaned forward to fix Sheriff Woods's wide-eyed stare. 'Now I appreciate what yuh done, Ed, and I know it's been yuh best. Wouldn't have doubted it. But it ain't enough, not for me it ain't. I seen them fellas, not for long, but I seen 'em and I heard 'em. No names, just voices, shapes, faces. Ain't likely to forget 'em neither, so wherever they are out there,

I'm walkin' in their shadows — for just as long as it takes to see 'em into Hell. Rest of my life if need be.'

The man eased back. 'That's the truth of it, Ed, and I'm pullin' out at noon.'

'Fellas yuh can't name, on a trail yuh can't find, could be anywhere . . . Hell, Tom, and just supposin' yuh do get to crossin' the rats, what then? Their sort ain't no soft bellies who just happened on gettin' high-spirited for a day. They're killers, professionals, vermin livin' by the gun and whatever their twisted minds get to schemin'.' Ed cleared another glistening of sweat from his face. 'How in hell yuh goin' to handle 'em, Tom, and you standin' by y'self at that? How yuh goin' to do it, eh? Take some lessons in fast shootin' or somethin'?'

'Might at that,' said the man crossing to the door. 'Or hand some out.'

'And just what's that supposed to mean, damn yuh?'

But by then the man had gone and

Sheriff Ed Woods was alone in a sticky, airless office with the door standing open to a sticky, airless street where even the flies were resting up.

And all he could summon to mouth to himself, the street, the town and its flies and the man already striding out to the livery, was: 'Hell!'

It seemed fitting.

2

Tom Huckerman left Trulso at noon that day in a ragbag of second-hand clothes, nothing in his pocket and riding a borrowed mount. Much, he thought, as he had ridden in all those years back.

Maggie McHay at the rooming-house had provided the clothes. 'Don't know who last stood in 'em — some fella down on his luck from way back, I guess, I get 'em all — but yuh welcome to 'em, Tom Huckerman. Fit where they touch, but, hell, they ain't holed that bad, and they're warm. Just don't bring 'em back, yuh hear?'

Curtis Oates, liveryman, part-time undertaker, with a notion he had missed his mark in life and should have been a preacher, had offered a mount without hesitation. 'Know yuh situation, Tom, and I gotta fair figurin' on what yuh plannin'. Do the same m'self. Who wouldn't? But I gotta say . . . Damnit, why should I? Man finds himself where you're standin' ain't for no persuadin' other, is he? I wish yuh well, and may the Good Lord ride with yuh. Hell, yuh goin' to need Him! Meantime, yuh got a fine mare here and my second-best saddle. Few supplies we rustled up between us. Scant enough, but can't do more, save pray . . . '

Sheriff Woods stood along of a dozen or so gathered outside the saloon to watch the man leave.

'Gotta hand it to the fella, he ain't short on guts,' murmured one.

'Wouldn't be sittin' where he is for a wagon of gold,' said another.

'Just hope that gal of his ain't — ' began a third.

'Don't even think it, fella,' drawled Ed, wondering how it was Tom Huckerman reckoned on handing out the 'fast shooting' without so much as a gunbelt buckled at his waist.

Maybe he should have asked. Maybe not.

★   ★   ★

There was the first whip of a freshening wind from the north threatening night rain by the time Tom reached the plain and slowed the mare to a canter before reining instinctively for the burned-out shell of the homestead.

The weeks spent living with the agony of his gashed, bruised body and the endless turmoil of images from the day of the raid had only stiffened his resolve not to turn his back on the blackened earth and skeleton of the grim reality of a month past.

'Day'll come when yuh'll be back there on that plain,' Maggie McHay had said on a night when she had sat at his bedside in the rooming-house, calming the rage of his pain and fever. 'Come soon enough too, I reckon. Then what yuh goin' to do? Ride on by, fool y'self that day didn't never happen? Tell

13

y'self it was all a bad, mad dream and there weren't no scumbags tearin' yuh life to pieces? The hell yuh will, Tom Huckerman! Them ashes ain't been scattered on the wind out there for nothin', and what's still standin' of them charred timbers yuh called home ain't there to no point.'

She had paused to take his hand in hers. 'Yuh'll get y'self out there, yuh hear? Soon as yuh able. Go pay yuh respects to May, and when yuh had that quiet moment, you and her, yuh get y'self fired up to go find that daughter of yours. Yuh understand? 'Cus that's what yuh gotta do, Tom Huckerman, that's yuh destiny from this night on. And there won't be no turnin' back, not never. Not 'til yuh done whatever's to be done and them ashes rest easy where they lie.

'Yuh pay heed to my words, fella, pay close heed, and when the wind comes a-whisperin' through that place and sniggers up all that dead dust and the ragbag pieces of the past 'til it seems like there's a hauntin' passin' through yuh, mebbe it'll tell yuh somethin', eh? Mebbe yuh'll get to hearin' the voices reachin' for yuh, tellin' yuh . . .

'And then yuh can ride on, Tom Huckerman. Yuh'll know where yuh goin'.'

★   ★   ★

There were already long evening shadows and swirls of parched dirt on the wind when Tom Huckerman turned again and reached the outcrop of gnarled rock and brush at the far end of the plain where it lifted for the foothills of the Broken Necks.

Place looked and felt as remote as ever, he thought, reining to a halt at the steepest side of the crop; hardly changed one mite in the dozen years since he had last stood in its shadow. But, then, that had been the whole point in finding the spot — somewhere anonymous, insignificant, as plain ordinary and unwelcome as the rest of the

Godforsaken sprawl going nowhere.

He grunted as he dismounted, hitched the mare and moved closer to the rock face. Damn it, he felt as guilty this night as he had those years back. It had been no way for a grown man, and newly wedded at that, to behave then, and he still had the sweaty sensation in the nape of his neck that May was looking over his shoulder even now.

Only difference being this time she would be nodding her approval.

He sank slowly to his knees and reached carefully through the dry, crackling brush to the hidden cleft at the foot of the rock, the sweat in his neck chillingly real.

His fingers worked softly, like insects teasing out a new home, then faster until they were delving deep into the recesses of the cleft. Supposing some two-bit drifter with nothing better to do, or something to hide, had holed up here by chance, he was thinking. That sort of thing happened; no-hopers got lucky, struck their own version of 'gold' on a whim, an instinctive nosiness for rummaging where no other man would rest his butt. Supposing this fellow . . .

His fingers settled easy on the bundle. His eyes closed and he heaved a long sigh of relief. No drifter, no chance probing. It was here, safe and dry as the day he had laid it to rest. 'Thank God,' he murmured, and drew the bundle through the brush and dirt to his knees.

There were minutes then when Tom Huckerman simply stared at the long-hidden package, tight in the rope still binding it, the dust cocooning it like some ancient membrane, and let his fingers move over the dried oil cloth as if easing it back to life, waiting for the first beat of a sleeping pulse.

Sun-up at Pickford and the shooting of Frank Coyne, the late noon show-down at Stand Bluff with the Ristoff boys; the night raid through Semblance, bank heist at Clifton, brush with Long Hair and the marauding Sioux; riding along of the Kavanagh bunch at the Stony Creek ambush; the stage hold-up out of Redfern, deep in Dakota territory, May stepping down to the dirt trail and looking him straight in the eye like she had been expecting him all her life, and his Colts that day handling heavy as wet rocks in his grip . . .

'Hell, May,' he murmured again, his fingers resting on the bundle, 'that was all a whole world away.' He grunted. 'And you there thinkin' after we were wed I was all through with them ways. And so I was, so I was, on my word. No goin' back, not after we hit Trulso and Holly came along and, damn it, we tried to lick that land to shape. Hell . . . '

He sighed. 'All through — 'ceptin' for the guns, May. Remember the day I went roundin' up that stray hog? Well, it weren't strayin' none. I was out here, buryin' this bundle. The guns, May, the same Colts I was fixin' on yuh mornin' we met. And they're right here now, in this old cloth, sound as ever. Mebbe yuh knew that all along, eh? Mebbe that's why yuh smiled like yuh did when

18

I said as how I'd put 'em to the price of the wagon.

'Well, I'm sorry — sorry I lied to yuh. Shouldn't have done that. But I ain't sorry one bit for what I did. Always figured there might come a time when I'd need these guns. Fella don't step outa my life as it was and lose that instinct. And we sure as damn it need 'em now, May. Yuh know that, don't yuh?'

Tom Huckerman had the gunbelt at his waist, the twin Colts holstered, and was mounted up and turning from the outcrop to the gathering night when he paused to scan the silhouetted peaks of the Broken Necks before breaking to the trail due north.

The man with the guns was back.

3

It rained, hard and wind-lashed, through that night as Tom Huckerman and his mount picked their way through the foothills of the mountain range, their trail directly north, with no detours, not even when inviting cover beckoned.

'North,' he murmured repeatedly, and sometimes a deal louder in the grip of a heavy downpour and the ice-edged rush of the wind that followed in its wake. And why north, he asked himself more than once? No good reason that even a sharp-eyed, wide-awake fellow might fathom from what he could make out in the rain-washed track at his feet. Nothing there that told of other mounts and men passing through, and certainly not a whole month back; just dirt trickling to dark mud that would bake to faceless sprawls come sun-up and the day's full heat.

It was north for Tom Huckerman on two counts: one, because six crazed fellows trailing a kidnapped twelve year old would ride, almost without knowing it themselves, for the deepest, remotest heart of the peaks. The Ristoff boys had done just that at Stand Bluff — gone deep, gone dark, like sated rats to a hidden lair — and that had been their big mistake.

Instinct was not always a trusty bedfellow.

And two, Maggie McHay, in that wrinkled, gnarled old way of hers, had been right. Standing there on the stained earth of his burned-out home had summoned to his mind all the voices he had needed to hear. Ghosts of his own making, the voices of obsession? Maybe, but they had spoken clear enough that afternoon in Pickford to warn him of the second gun buried in the folds of Frank Coyne's dust-coat.

Fellow could get to trusting voices that good.

And, hell, he had reasoned, through the darkest, wettest hours of that night, with the wind like a cold blade on his back and his sodden clothes squelching to every shift of the mount's steps, was there any other way? North was as sound right now as east or west.

Just a darned sight steeper!

★   ★   ★

It was the pitching roll of thunder and the crack of lightning that finally drove the man to shelter in the half-dry cover of a rocky overhang an hour before first light.

Time to rest the mare, dry out best he could, stretch his aching limbs, close his eyes in the twitchy doze that would soon fill the darkness with the shapes and sweat of those same haunting faces: the dirt and stubble-shadowed masks of the raiders, the drained look of fear and despair in Holly's last stare, the soft smile at May's lips in the tightening grip of death, Maggie McHay's watchful gaze through the lantern-lit gloom of the rooming-house; gunslingers, bar girls, lawmen from what might have been a hundred years long past . . .

He twitched into life again at the sudden snort of the mare, conscious of his fingers slipping as if through a sixth sense to the butts of his Colts.

He grunted and eased his sodden shirt from the rock face.

Been close to what some would reckon a lifetime since Tom Huckerman had last handled Colts. Them days, back there at Semblance, Stony Creek and a dozen other places where the gun played the game and the blaze of it spat the rules, he had been fast, sharp as cactus with an edge that never failed. He grunted again. But that had been ten years ago. What of now, today? Would there be that same snap, the same unblinking reaction when it seemed the gun had been there in his fingers from birth? Or would he . . .

23

Damn it, he would get to knowing soon enough. Meantime, the rain was easing, storm passing to the west and a new day sliding over the eastern peaks smooth as untouched silk. A fine day for some hard tracking, he was thinking, when the scream echoed through the hills like another haunting.

But not of his making.

★   ★   ★

Tom waited, listening, wondering if the silence would crack again, then edged carefully from the overhang to the mud-skimmed track fronting it. He blinked on the soft glimmerings of light where it slipped over the still wet rocks, and slid his gaze slowly to his surroundings.

Sheer rock to his back, boulders thick as muscles to left and right, but ahead of him, on a shale and loose rock slope, the drop to a creek hidden in the shroud of morning mist breathing through it.

24

The scream had come from down there, he thought, tightening his gaze on the grey swirl; a woman's scream, high pitched from a throat in the grip of real fear. But now, only silence. Not so much as the shift of a pebble. Nothing, save the mist and somewhere back of him the drip of gathered rain to mud.

He swallowed, rested a hand on the butt of a Colt, checked that the mare was still loose hitched, and eased the few steps to the edge of the mist shroud.

Could just do nothing, of course, he reasoned, feeling for safe footholds; sit it out right there in the overhang till either the woman screamed again, or not. The hell he could! Or maybe he had been mistaken. Maybe the scream had been the screech of a hawk at the kill. The hell it had! That scream . . .

It pitched again, high and echoing, at first shrill as if on a spiral of escape to the peaks, then thickening to a groan that gurgled in a grip of pain.

Tom waited, sweating now, his eyes

aching in his probing stare. Damn it, there was nothing to see, not so much as the vaguest blur of a shape down there — and *down there* might be one hell of a drop to nowhere!

He risked another foothold, another, a half-dozen, conscious of the softest shift of dirt, grateful that the night rain was binding it for now.

He passed into the thicker mist, shivered at the damp chill of its touch, squinted, moved on, reached the cover of an outcrop boulder and dropped behind it. What now? Just wait, listen, risk going on? A fast shot into the mist might settle the issue, at least signal to whoever was down there that another body was about. 'Yeah,' he muttered to himself on a cloud of white breath, 'and draw a whole blaze of lead in return!'

One more step, maybe to the right, and he might just . . . He froze at the croak of a curse. Man's voice. Bad tempered, in no mood to reason. Quaking murmur from the woman. The crunch of a boot over pebbles. Another string of curses. A sob, a scramble. More crunching.

Tom Huckerman was clear of the boulder, a Colt tight in his hand, and scattering dirt down the slope in one decisive shift.

He tumbled through the mist cloud, his free hand clawing over rock, legs and feet kicking into shale, felt the damp like a wet cloth across his face, and seemed for shattering seconds to be falling forever before breaking into streaky slivers of grey light, slithering to a halt and smelling the sweat even then of the man only yards away.

Barn-door bulk of a fellow, heavy-chested, tree-trunk thighs and legs, with a face like a pitted copper pan, eyes as sharp as stones, a half grin, half leer cracking the parched lips bulging through black stubble. And at the man's back, her body sprawled across the shale as if washed up there on some flash flood, the woman, or what, in that first quick glance, Tom could still recognize as being something vaguely female.

'Where in hell — ?' barked the man, swinging the misted glint of a Winchester into Tom's face.

Fellow was in two minds about taking the pressure on that trigger, thought Tom, straining to keep a steady hold on his Colt, too surprised and bewildered right now to be certain of what to do, of just who it was had crashed out of the dawn like some hangover of nightmare, but it was going to take him no more than the seconds of a closer glare to figure he preferred his own company.

Tom slid another glance at the woman, caught the shivering fear in her stare, watched her fingers grasping aimlessly at stone, the blood from the cuts across her neck and temple trickle over the bruising that disappeared into the folds of the rags that passed for clothes.

'Lady there looks to be in need of some attention,' he murmured, his gaze flattening on the man's face.

'She ain't your business, mister,' croaked the man, gesturing the rifle a shade closer and higher.

'Wouldn't reckon that,' said Tom. 'No, wouldn't say that at all. She needs lookin' to.' He was easing upright as the man crunched a step forward.

'Keep yuh nose out and yuh hands off, fella, unless yuh want me to leave yuh here without either. Just git while yuh still able.' The rifle prodded again. 'Yuh got it?'

'Oh, sure,' drawled Tom, still easing upright. 'I read yuh like a book.' He smiled as he reached his full height, then spat between the man's straddled legs. 'Nasty!' he mouthed.

The Colt blazed once from Tom Huckerman's hip; twice as he took the kick and steadied the aim; a third time, levelled and at arm's length, to burn a hole dead centre of the barn-door bulky fellow's stone-glazed eyes.

'Just like it was for Frank Coyne,' he murmured, then turned and crunched his way to the shuddering woman.

4

Seemed like only yesterday — waiting and watching on somebody who might or might not make it. Every next breath, every flicker of an eyelid, they all counted, gave the body a fighting chance.

May Huckerman had run clean out of chances all those years back at the homestead, but this woman, whoever she was, however she had come to be in the hands of the scumbag stiffening to crow meat at the foot of the creek, was going to make it, thought Tom, easing from her side in the soft morning shade of the overhang.

Sure she was, he mused, given time and the care of someone with not much else to do. He hardly fitted the role; no time and a whole lot more to get to before the dawning of many more days.

So, he grunted, where to now?

Wait for the woman to recover and be able to ride, or move her as she was to some place safe? And just where in the wilderness of the Broken Necks was he going to find that? Sure as hell not round the next twist of track, far side of the nearest peak!

Should he turn back to Trulso, head for the Smithson spread east side of the plain, or just wait, damn it, till she could tell him where she hailed from and simply take her home? Might be presuming a whole lot more than was healthy in that; 'home' was as likely as not the last place she would want to see again if that was where her nightmare had begun. And just where, he wondered, had that been anyhow?

Not a deal to be gleaned from the mounts he had rounded up; couple of mangy bedrolls, worn, holed blanket, canteens, pack of jerky, bag of beans, coffee, battered pot and two mugs, half a bottle of mescal, dirt, dust and not much else. Fellow had either been travelling light or clean out of luck.

He was clean out of everything now, Tom had thought, collecting the man's Winchester as he had stepped clear of the body. Too slow in his reckoning; too tight in his grip on the rifle; too thick-headed and lathered up to see the look in Tom's eyes. Always follow a fellow's eyes if you wanted to measure the pressure on his trigger finger. It was the eyes . . .

He had stopped then, stiffened, breathed long and deep and heavy there in the mist, felt the chill of cold sweat in his neck, the twitch of his fingers. He was back — oh, yes, he was back, the old-times Tom Huckerman with Colts in his hands and a stare that could strip a fellow to the bone; the reckoning gunslinger who 'read' a man and followed his eyes, listened to the voices in his head and rated a dead man no better, no worse, than the dirt where he lay.

He had shivered, his thoughts spinning through images of May and the day she had handed him their child right there in the homestead. 'New life, Tom,' she had smiled. 'Let's make it good for her . . . '

Damn it, standing here waiting on the fate of a woman who might be anybody from almost anywhere, whose only hold on his life had come in the piercing echo of a scream, was no place to be when there was his daughter out there waiting on her own fate and maybe wondering even now if this would be the last morning she would get to seeing.

And then the woman had stirred and spoken.

★ ★ ★

'Dori Maguire,' she murmured, struggling to sit upright, her back to the rock, hands fluttering to the rags of her clothing. 'Sorry I ain't at my best.' She smiled fitfully, fingers moving over the stragglings of her hair. 'Must look a rare sight.'

Tom shifted a step closer. 'Take it

easy there. Yuh ain't in no fit state — '

'Don't have to tell me, mister. I feel it every place I got! Some I didn't know to!' She winced, squirmed against the rock and winced again. 'I owe yuh,' she said, running a hand over a thigh. 'That I surely do, whoever yuh are.'

'I just happened — ' began Tom.

'So yuh did at that. And yuh shoot real fast with it.' She halted the soothing hand and glanced quickly, anxiously into Tom's eyes. 'Yuh some sharp gunslinger or somethin'?'

'One time, way back,' murmured Tom.

'Well, yuh ain't lost yuh touch. I'll vouch for that. Ain't seen a fella take another out that way since . . . Don't matter. That sonofabitch got his full measure. Damn his eyes!' The woman winced again and let the soothing hand slip to her back. 'Hell!' she hissed. 'Reckon Stotts must've tramped all over me.'

'Stotts?' frowned Tom.

'No good, two-bit fella yuh just shot.

34

Drunken drifter. A nobody out of no place, save maybe Hell.' The woman grinned softly. 'Didn't give him time to introduce himself, did yuh? Yuh didn't miss much. He had that comin'.'

'Mebbe,' said Tom impatiently. 'I ain't for seein' a fella handlin' a woman that way. How come yuh were tied in with him, anyhow?'

'Long story, mister, but in a spit, he won me.'

'*Won yuh!*'

'Card game. Poker. Sonofabitch held a big hand for once in his miserable life. Stakes got high. I was top of the heap.' Dori Maguire winced again, sighed and shrugged. 'And in case yuh gettin' too polite to ask, you're right — bar girl, that's me. Nothin' more, nothin' less. Don't make no apology for it. Way of the world. Drew a short straw or somethin'. Too late then, too late now.' She paused, her expression as bland as the rock at her back. 'Yuh came to the aid of a tart, mister, a whore, that's the plain fact of it.'

Tom held the woman's stare, then grunted softly and turned to gaze over the shimmer of dust and dirt to the sunlit peaks. 'A woman, ma'am,' he said quietly. 'I helped a woman. Don't see it no other.'

There were moments then of a silence that seemed to drift between them like some leftover of the early mist, Dori Maguire watching Tom Huckerman's back, Tom with his gaze narrowed on the twisting fingers of track through the mountains.

'Yeah, well,' said the woman at last, 'I guess we all got shadows back of our bones, y'self included. So what's a one-time gunslinger doin' out here with what don't look to be no more than a pair of fancy Colts and what he stands in? Or ain't yuh sayin?'

★ ★ ★

He was, beginning, 'My name's Huckerman, Tom Huckerman,' then telling it slow and steady, in flat, matter-of-fact tones, his voice seemingly detached from emotion, his gaze still fixed on the tracks through the far peaks. Telling it just as it had happened from the first dust-hazed sight of the raiders crossing the plain in the blaze of the noon sun, to their last yell, the beat of hoofs, the hiss and crackle of the burning homestead, the hollow, haunting pitch of Holly's screams. Telling it as much to himself as the woman seated back of him who listened in silence, without a word or comment, until he was all through, down to the merest detail and his voice drained away to an empty whisper.

'Rough, that's real rough, mister,' said Dori Maguire breaking the tight silence. 'Rough as it gets, I guess. Thanks for tellin' me, but I reckon yuh needed to, eh? Get it off yuh chest. Makes a body feel a whole lot better, 'spite of the hurt.' She stifled a sigh through a grimaced wince. 'Can't say I blame yuh for what yuh doin', but, hell, yuh got y'self some search there. Tell yuh somethin', though, if that gal's ma is some place where she can see yuh right now, she'd be back of yuh, mister, every step of the way.' She sighed again, this time freely. 'Don't need me to tell you that. Fact is, yuh don't need me, end of story. Just wastin' yuh time. So if yuh'd get me to a horse.'

'And just where yuh plannin' on goin', ma'am?' said Tom, turning quickly. 'Like I say, yuh ain't in no fit state — '

'Oh, don't you fret y'self none on my account, Tom Huckerman. I been in worse fixes — not quite so painful, mebbe, but tight enough. Story of my life. Outa one pan, straight into whatever fire's goin'!' The woman smiled as she eased to her knees. 'I'll be just fine. Amazin' what a day without that sonofabitch Stotts manhandlin' me'll do. Won't know me come sundown. Get m'self washed some-place, cut a poncho from that blanket, saddle up and ride . . . ' She paused, frowning. 'Yeah, well, that might take some considerin'.'

'Yuh got a home?' asked Tom.

'Mister, I ain't had so much as a stick of 'home' as yuh put it since I was knee-high to a midge, and that's fact. I known only scumbags' cabins, back of cattle-drive wagons, whores' huts and two-bit saloons. There ain't never been nothin' else. Fella leadin' the life yuh once led'd know what I'm sayin'. Bet yuh seen my sort a thousand times, eh? Sure yuh have. I ain't for hidin' nothin', not this late on.'

'So where'd Stotts win yuh?'

'Back there, ten, mebbe a dozen miles into the Broken Necks. Trail dump run by a fella name of Brenard. Saloon-cum-store-cum-anything-yuh-choose sorta place, suitin' just about every dirt-dredged roughneck drifter and no-gooder yuh could lay a name to. Brenard grabbed me outa North Forks.' The woman shrugged. 'It happens. Too damned often! So I guess — '

'This place,' murmured Tom, his eyes suddenly dark and narrowed, 'yuh say it's on the trail. Headin' where?'

'God knows! As deep into them hills and mountains as yuh'd care to risk, I guess. Never got to askin'.'

Tom's gaze stayed narrowed. 'Yuh didn't by chance happen to see while yuh were there — '

'Now just hold it, mister,' said Dori, coming to her feet and reaching to the rock face for support. 'I'm gettin' yuh drift. You're thinkin' that mebbe them fellas holdin' — yuh daughter . . . Hell, that's about as thin a straw to cling to as — '

'Lady, I ain't got nothin' else right now. If there's somebody — anybody out here who might've seen somethin' of Holly, then I'm for gettin' to 'em, fast as I can.'

'Yuh goin' down there,' croaked Dori, 'to see Brenard?'

'I am, just as soon as I got you sorted, ma'am.'

'Sorted be damned! T'ain't me who needs sortin', mister, it's you! Take yuh three days to find that place, *if* yuh got lucky. And then some. T'ain't exactly sign-posted! If that's where yuh goin', and yuh set on it, then yuh goin' to need me. I owe yuh that much. So just hand me that blanket there, eh? Time I got to lookin' somethin' like decent for once!'

5

They trailed hard into the Broken Necks through that day, their mounts struggling and heaving against the baked scatterings of the narrow tracks, their limbs and bodies taut to staying seated, the sweat across them thick and hot as axle grease.

Dori Maguire had laid out the plan with a flourish of her arms beneath the makeshift poncho. 'I lead, mister, and you stay close bringin' up Stotts' mount. No springin' to yuh own path. T'ain't safe, 'specially when we hit the higher drift. Should make Belly Creek come dusk. Mountain stream close by. And that'll be it for t'day. Horses won't take no more.'

Tom had nodded his ready agreement; the woman, after all, knew the way to Brenard's and that, slim though the chance of learning more of the raiders might prove, was all that counted for now. He would know when the show was back on his range.

Meantime . . . Some woman, he thought and murmured more than once through those stifling, high sun hours. No doubting it. Whatever the pain, however great the effort, Dori Maguire, dirt-smudged and dishevelled, was game for it. And no complaining. Maybe she never did. Who, in her way of life, would be listening anyhow?

But once at Brenard's place, what then? Would she dare show herself? Would she want to? And later, when Tom had drained the mountain lair of whatever it had to offer — more likely drawn a blank and could only move on — where would Dori Maguire be heading?

Hell, he thought, just supposing he had picked up a shadow there was no shaking off. Supposing Dori Maguire . . .

'No fire when we hit the creek,' she had called. 'We eat and drink cold.

Brenard's got some nasty habits when he catches the smoke of squatters. Be warned, mister!'

Yes, ma'am, he had grinned to himself, recalling for no good reason he could imagine the night raid at Semblance all those years back.

★ ★ ★

'Yuh serious about them scum bringin' yuh daughter this way?' said the woman when they were settled at the creek stream in the sprawl of the first night shadows. ' 'Cus I gotta tell yuh, mister, I sure as hell didn't see no such fellas at Brenard's before Stotts dragged me outa the dump. Nothin' like six of 'em with a gal that age. Could hardly have missed 'em, could I?'

True enough, Tom had agreed, but suppose only two of the party had collected supplies and whatever else needed at Brenard's. Suppose the others had stayed out of sight with Holly. Suppose they had a 'customer' far down the trail waiting on delivery of her. Now just where might that be? Any notion?

'Not a spit of one,' Dori had shrugged. 'Far as I know, or care come to that, these mountains are as back-of-beyond as yuh can get. Wilderness, mister, plain as that. Nothin' out there worth liftin' an eyelid to note. Tell yuh somethin', though,' she had added, her gaze on Tom darkening, 'if them rats did come this way, and assumin' yuh gal was still anythin' like breathin', they wouldn't be plannin' on holdin' to her for long. Gal that age needs lookin' to proper if she's goin' to fetch a price, and six of the type I figure these scum for ain't exactly qualified in motherly attention. Plain fact, mister. They'll want to unload her fast, get shut of her, collect the money and ride. I know. I been there.'

Dori Maguire had come slowly to her feet then, her hands brushing absent-mindedly at the worn blanket poncho. 'I was just fourteen when I got took,'

45

she murmured, her gaze settling on the slow swirl of the stream. 'Sorta thing yuh ain't likely to forget.'

She had waited only a moment to shrug, murmur softly to herself, stiffen and wade almost without a shiver into the ice-cold mountain flow.

Minutes later she was out of the poncho and washing the trail dirt from her body when Tom tipped his hat over his eyes and lay back on his saddle pillow.

Trail dirt you could wash clear, Tom thought. Memories stuck.

★   ★   ★

It was deep into the night, with the moon still full and round and the starlight at its brightest in a cloudless sky, when Tom slid from the nightmare of screams and flame and lay instinctively still in a lathering of sweat at the sound that had jerked him awake.

A mount's snort; the softest shift in the thickest shadows of loose rock;

silence, another shift, a hushed, stifled curse. Silence again.

Tom's eyes flicked anxiously to the sleeping shape of the woman. Tight in her own dreams, or otherwise, he thought, his body relaxed now, limbs easy, ears primed for the next soft shift. Stay that way, leastways for just as long as it was going to take for the stalking bush-whacker out there to get real careless.

And he would, he surely would, same as they all did when it seemed the pickings were going to be easy. But how many of them, he wondered? More than one for sure, but maybe only two; pair of slip-witted drifters out of food, money, looking for a simple lift of anything, specially mounts and guns, that would fetch the price of a bottle at a place like Brenard's.

Could be the pair had been tracking them most of the day, sitting back there waiting on nightfall, reckoning on one man and a poncho-frocked woman hardly likely to break more than a sliver of their mangy sweat.

The sort of thinking that led to anxious boots overlooking loose rock, the straggle of brush that cracked like a whip in the still of night.

So ease on, fellow, ease on . . .

Another snort as the mount's unease grew, another hissed curse, the scuff of a boot over dried brush. Silence. The fellow was making a poor job of this; probably waiting on his partner now, one eye on the sleeping bodies, wondering how deep their sleep, how fast they would have to move to make it permanent. Knife job, thought Tom. They would be trusting to the flash of a blade at an exposed throat. Done it before, they could do it again. All a question of timing, holding the silence.

Damn it, Dori Maguire was stirring! A half groan, a throaty gulp, twitch of the legs, one arm reaching out, fingers flat on the cold rock. If she woke now, one of the stalkers would have to move. No choice, save to pull back in the misery of a whole day's effort wasted. No chance.

A shape, far side of a cluster of boulders at the stream. Hefty fellow, crouched low, motionless, simply waiting. Maybe he figured he had the time. Why rush it; plenty of night to come yet?

Dori had slipped back to deep sleep, the arm like something discarded, fingers dead as a broken claw. Now was the moment for the hefty fellow to make his move. Four fast, cat-soft steps and he would be mantling the woman with the blade poised tight and steady, all set to do its grisly worst.

But not tonight, fellow, thought Tom, tensing where he lay, his eyes wide open, thin line of sweat gleaming in the stubble of a moustache, not tonight. And maybe not for all the nights in Creation to come.

Tom Huckerman rolled like a log kicked into sudden life, one hand already gripping the butt of a gleaming Colt that blazed low and vicious while his body was still flat to the rock. The hefty fellow stood his ground for just seconds, eyes white as scrubbed plates, his arms spread, one hand tight on the knife, and stared at Tom as if seeing a ghost.

The fellow mouthed something nobody heard as blood oozed through his shirt and his eyes rolled into nowhere still not certain of who or what they had seen.

Tom spun where he lay to catch the sight of Dori Maguire on her knees and the thickening bulk of the second stalker thudding towards him.

The Colt blazed again, this time in a levelled streak of fire that spun the man like a crazed top and sent his blade clattering into rocks as he groaned and gripped torn flesh at his shoulder.

He was face-down in his own blood, but still breathing, when Tom stood over him and buried a boot deep in his ribs. 'Clumsy,' he murmured, and spat.

6

'Light sleeper, ain't yuh?' Dori Maguire hugged the poncho to her against the night chill and shivered. 'Hell, that was close!' She shivered again. 'He goin' to live?' she asked through chattering teeth as she peered at the wounded stalker. 'Don't look healthy.'

'He'll live,' said Tom, holstering the Colt with a satisfied thrust. 'God knows why.'

'Say,' frowned Dori shuffling a step closer to the man, 'don't I know him from some place? Ugly face looks kinda familiar.' She shuffled again until she had the fellow's features clear in the moonlight. 'I know him. Don't I just! Mohawk Stein as ever was, and that must be his partner, Fletch Bono, yuh put to rest. Customers back at Brenards. Scumbags. Bet they been

51

sittin' on my butt since Stotts pulled out.'

Tom grunted, then dragged the groaning man to the foot of a boulder and propped him up. 'That so?' he croaked, leaning into the fellow's creased, sweat-streaked face. 'Yuh been followin' the lady here?'

'She ain't no lady,' moaned the man through a wince that bubbled the sweat on his cheeks. 'She's — ' He choked on the thud of Tom's boot into his thigh, rolled his eyes and grabbed at a surge of pain through his shoulder. 'Damn yuh!'

'You do that, fella,' said Tom squatting in the scratch of light. 'T'ain't goin' to do yuh a mite of good. So now yuh get to apologizin' to the lady, eh? Do somethin' decent for once, unless, o'course, yuh want me — '

'Hold it,' murmured Dori, still shivering as she stepped closer. 'He ain't no use to us dead.'

'Ain't nothin' to us alive,' quipped Tom.

'Could be,' said Dori. She hugged the poncho to her and settled a deep gaze on Stein's face. 'Yuh been busy, Mohawk?' she asked quietly. 'How'd yuh figure this? Yuh figure on liftin' me outa Stotts's hands for yuh own use? That it? Sell me on next two-bit town yuh hit? Whose idea, yours or Bono's? He ain't sayin'.'

The man merely licked his lips and glared.

'Well, don't matter none now, does it? Yuh lost out, and I'm for reckonin' on my good friend here bein' kinda anxious to be rid of yuh. Hell, yuh would've knifed us a half-hour back! Yuh gotta pay for that, ain't yuh? Only reasonable, unless, o'course, we find a use for yuh.'

Stein's glare tightened, white and wet in the moon's flitting light.

'Seems to me, yuh bein' such a reg'lar customer at Brenard's place, yuh would've had yuh eyes rattler-skinned as ever for any new faces passin' through. That right, Mohawk?'

53

The man winced and grunted.

'Sure yuh would,' smiled Dori. 'Always lookin' for a liftin', ain't yuh? Second nature. Well, now, you just cast that half-wit mind of yours back some to strangers ridin' in — two mebbe, three, kinda in a hurry. 'Bout a month back or thereabouts. Might've been loose-lipped about havin' a young gal along of 'em.' She paused. 'Mean anythin', Mohawk? Yuh gettin' a flicker of recollection in what passes for yuh brain?'

Tom Huckerman swallowed and leaned closer, his eyes bright and narrowed.

'Go to hell!' spat Stein.

'Suit y'self,' shrugged Dori, with a sudden swirl of the poncho. 'T'ain't worth a cuss either way. Might as well finish it now. Night air's gettin' lean.' She nodded at Tom, then winked as she half-turned. 'Do it, mister,' she snapped. 'One sure shot. In the head. And hurry, f'Crissake!'

Tom drew a Colt and eased the

hammer through a long, deliberate click.

Stein winced, watched the gun, then the trickle of blood through his fingers at the wound.

Dori Maguire snuggled deeper into the poncho, lifted her eyes to the high, yellow moon and began to hum.

'Fella with a scar side of his face,' mouthed Stein, saliva dribbling to his stubble. 'Tall, long-legged, black pants. Had a coupla gunhands with him.'

'Name?' snapped Dori.

'Didn't give none,' croaked Stein.

'What about a girl?' said Tom, beginning to sweat. 'What he say about her?'

'Never said nothin' 'bout a gal. On my word he didn't. Just gave me this. Said it'd raise the price of a bottle.' Stein's free hand fumbled at the pocket of his shirt, the fingers working anxiously until they settled, waited, then slowly, like nervous worms, drew a crucifix and chain to the light. 'This,' mumbled Stein. 'Fella gave me this.'

Tom holstered the Colt, took the cross and dropped it to the palm of his hand. 'It's hers,' he murmured. 'It's Holly's. Present from her ma.'

'Where'd these fellas go?' snapped Dori again. 'And don't give me them 'weren't notin'' lies. Yuh'd be watchin', sure enough. Which way? Where to?'

'Didn't name a place,' said Stein, glancing hurriedly at Tom. 'Just north.' He coughed on a pinched throat. 'Could be anywhere. Ain't no town worth callin' such 'til yuh hit Morton, and that ain't nothin' but a ghost.' He coughed again. 'But I never set eyes on no gal, and that's the truth. And nobody said nothin'.'

'Yuh sure about names?' asked Tom.

'No names. Fellas just rode in, took what they wanted and left. Tall fella dropped that in my hand as he passed. Must've figured I could use it.'

'To pray with right now!' sneered Dori. She huddled into the poncho again and turned to Tom. 'Don't tell yuh the gal's still alive, does it?' she murmured staring at the crucifix in his hand. 'But yuh can be sure them rats came this way. Yuh were right about that. What about the fella with the scar? He mean anything?'

'He was one of 'em,' said Tom softly. 'He rounded up Holly. I seen him.' His fingers closed on the cross and chain. 'Yuh know this Morton place?' he asked.

'No, never set eyes on the heap. Don't sound much. On the other hand . . . ' Dori's gaze narrowed in concentration. 'Sorta place them fellas might head for 'til the heat's off. Could rest up there easy enough and then move on. Outa sight, deep in the mountains, in a one-time town . . . Sounds about right.' She paused and opened her eyes wide on Tom's face. 'That where yuh headin'?'

'Best I got right now,' said Tom. 'Ain't goin' to learn nothin' new at Brenard's.'

'Count me along of yuh?' grinned Dori with a sudden flourish of the poncho. 'I ain't got no other place in mind, and 'sides, I owe yuh again for sleepin' light! What about Mohawk here? We finish him?'

'Leave him,' said Tom flatly. 'No boots, no horse. Nothin'. If he wants to live, he'll figure a way. But as for yuh comin' along of me — '

'Don't let's get to arguin', mister. I had enough of a rousin' for one night! What yuh got there in yuh hand is a hope. Not a deal, but somethin'. And yuh got lucky. So have I. Mebbe it's only the start. Let's go see come first light, eh? Like yuh say, best we got right now.'

The crucifix bit deep into the flesh of Tom's hand as his grip on it sweated and tightened. 'Sure,' he croaked, 'let's go see.'

7

At about the time Tom Huckerman and Dori Maguire were trailing deeper due north into the Broken Necks through a first light still no more than a crack in the east, Sheriff Ed Woods was pulling on his boots and figuring on going nowhere.

He had no cause to, he reckoned. Town was quiet, folk along of it; jail was empty and likely to stay that way; the good were being just that, those inclined otherwise were sleeping it off, and there had not been so much as the shadow of a stranger through Trulso in days.

No, he decided, he could do nothing and go nowhere. A day for staying clear of the hell-fire sun and hugging the shade on the porch. Maybe treat himself to a fat cigar, measure of his best whiskey come noon, then ease away the hours to a quiet sundown.

But all that was before he had opened the door to the already shimmering haze of the street and blinked at the slow, lone rider trailing in from the south.

Fellow had come some distance, he thought, squinting against the early glare for a closer look. Clothes, hat and boots were dust-bitten to the last crease; mount had a worn look to it too. Nothing about the man he recognized, but, hell, that scorched, wind-slapped face, the quick, gleaming eyes that seemed to be everywhere, sure set the fellow apart — as did the fine-boned butt of the Colt just clearing the drift of his dustcoat.

Not, Sheriff Woods concluded, flicking his braces over his shoulders, a fellow to tangle with lightly. Leastways, not unless you happened to be the law hereabouts.

'Mornin',' he called, stepping to the edge of the boardwalk. 'I'd figure that for bein' a long night's ride, mister.'

'Yuh'd be right,' said the man, easing the tired mount to the hitching rail. 'Livery in town?' he asked, dismounting wearily.

'Curtis Oates, top end of the street. Best there is for a hundred miles — all there is for a hundred miles! He'll look to yuh horse well enough, mister. Throw in some liniment for y'self with it, seein' as how we ain't had a doc for five years.' Sheriff Woods slid his thumbs to his braces. 'Goin' far?' he asked, his gaze narrowing.

'Depends,' said the man as he patted and soothed the mount.

'On what?' quipped Ed quickly, the gaze tighter.

'On what I find here.'

'That'll be dependin' on what yuh lookin' for,' grinned Ed, lifting his braces. 'We ain't got a deal worth eyein'. Maggie McHay's roomin'-house; store and a bar back of it — don't open 'til ten; barberin' place — hot bath's extra; timber-yard, corral, handful of town folk. Mostly farmers hereabouts small-time and generally broke. Oh, and me.' Ed released the thumbs and twanged the braces flat to his shirt. 'I'm the law. Sheriff Woods.'

'Pleased to meet yuh,' murmured the man, still tending the mount.

'Likewise. Didn't catch yuh name.'

'Didn't give none.'

'No, but yuh goin' to,' said Ed, relaxing his weight to one leg. 'Ain't yuh?'

The man gave the mount a final pat and raised his eyes slowly, the stare intent on Sheriff Woods's face. 'Coyne,' he croaked. 'Marshal Coyne. Retired.'

'That so,' said Ed, his grin spreading again. 'Hell, why didn't yuh say straight off, f'Crissake? Don't get to clappin' eyes on a marshal too often, retired or otherwise. Fact, never seen a marshal, not since I was out Kansas way. Well, now, ain't this a day for sure? And me thinkin' there as how I'd be moochin' away the hours back of a cigar! Better still, share a smoke with yuh, Marshal — after yuh've had coffee and mebbe some breakfast, eh? Looks as if yuh could use it. And don't go frettin' none about that horse there. I'll get Curtis gathered in faster than yuh can spit. Yuh bet. Now, you just step up here, make y'self at home. Real welcome yuh are, and that's a fact.' Ed reached for a handshake. 'Got somethin' special yuh tendin' to this far west?' he asked.

'Just a whereabouts,' said the Marshal. 'Fella name of Huckerman. Tom Huckerman. Know him?'

★   ★   ★

'Let me get this straight, so's I ain't foolin' m'self into thinkin' I'm dreamin'.' Sheriff Woods slumped in his chair behind his desk, sighed, blinked, steepled his fingers to a sharp stubble at his chin, and stared through a deep frown at his early-morning visitor.

'Yuh tellin' me,' he began carefully, 'that you, brother of the one-time gunslingin' murderer, Frank Coyne, have spent these past three years since

63

yuh retired as a marshal back East, trackin' down the fella who shot yuh brother in a showdown at Pickford more than twelve years back just so yuh can *ask* him what really happened on that day, and that the fella standin' at that showdown was Tom Huckerman, himself a wanted man through a half-dozen midwest territories? That what yuh tellin' me? Mister, that takes some swallowin' no matter which way yuh offerin' it!'

Marshal Coyne shrugged behind the steaming mug of fresh coffee then levelled his gaze on the street beyond the open door. 'Mebbe,' he murmured, 'but that's how it is, and yuh got my word on it.'

'Oh, I ain't doubtin' yuh, Marshal,' said Ed, collapsing the fingers to his lap. 'No, I ain't sayin' as how yuh ain't right to the last spit and stop of what yuh tellin' me. I'm just *askin' myself* how it was a fella like Tom Huckerman could roll that wagon of his into town, pretty wife, May, along of him, build that place of theirs with their own hands, raise a kid and go through all he went through comin' to a head in what happened month or so back, and me, the law, wearin' the badge round here, never knowin' a thing, not a speck, of just who he really was! That's what I'm *askin'*, damn it!'

The marshal turned from the open door. 'Yuh didn't know 'cus yuh weren't meant to know,' he said quietly. 'Day Tom Huckerman lost his heart to a woman and hung up his guns was the day he went back to bein' plain Tom Huckerman.'

'Nothin' *plain* about Tom,' said Ed, settling his arms on the desk. 'Nossir, nothin' plain at all, leastways not to folk hereabouts. Sure, he and May lived a quiet life out there on the plain. Not given a deal to socializin', 'ceptin' when they came to town for supplies — and only then when they could pay for 'em. Tom weren't for runnin' to no credit lines — and, hell, there weren't a deal of time for bein' that neighbourly, not with the sorta spread they had. Only time they seen was for sweatin' and workin' and more sweatin'.' Ed stared blankly at the desktop. 'All sweat . . . Then Holly came along, bright as a pippit, a real good-looker same as her ma. And Tom, why, he doted on that gal like there weren't no other. Same after May died like she did that bad winter . . . ' He slapped the desk with a flat, thudding hand. 'Hell, Marshal, if that were a reformed, two-bit gun-slinger, I'd fill the town with 'em!'

'Sure yuh would,' said the marshal, 'but that don't — '

'Tell yuh somethin' else, and I ain't foolin' here.' Ed came slowly, deliberately to his feet, his stare sharp as a blade on Coyne's face. 'If I'd been half the sheriff I should've been the day Tom Huckerman rode outa here trackin' down them sonsofbitches who torched his place and snatched his gal, I'd have been right alongside him, all the way, for as long as it's goin' to take, far as it goes. That's what I should've done. Too damn late now.'

'But not too late for me.' The marshal slid the empty mug to the desk. 'I still got all the time there is.'

Ed stiffened, a line of sweat glistening on his brow. 'What is it with you, Marshal? Yuh got some bug nestin' in yuh or somethin'? Yuh get the bad draw of a brother sittin' wrong side of the fence to yuh — fella who dies in the dirt of his own makin' at the hand of one of his kind — and yuh wanna go *ask* his killer what happened! Hell, ain't it obvious? Tom Huckerman was faster, simple as that. What more do yuh want? Or is it revenge yuh lookin' for? That the way of it? This some sorta blood reckonin', family honour? This how yuh goin' to use up yuh *retirement*?' Ed brushed a hand over the sweat. 'Know somethin'? I'd get to askin' y'self if that brother of yours ain't rattlin' yuh bones and laughin' like a mule every time he hears 'em! He really worth it?'

The marshal crossed to the door, eased the folds of his dustcoat aside and slid a fast, gleaming gaze over the street. 'No,' he murmured, 'Frank weren't never worth a spit. Mebbe I'd have shot him m'self if we'd crossed. So mebbe all I really wanna do is thank this Tom Huckerman. Who knows? I ain't found him yet.'

'And a hell-to-a-hidin' yuh ever will up there in them mountains. They ain't no place for a fella to be longer than it takes to clear 'em. And as for that gal — '

'Huckerman packin' irons when he pulled out?' snapped the marshal, turning again.

'Not so much as a knife and fork,' sighed Ed. 'Never seen him wear a gun.'

The marshal grunted. 'Which ain't to say he sold them fancy pair he always toted, is it?'

'Yuh sayin' — ' began Ed.

'All I'm sayin', Sheriff, is my figurin' on Tom Huckerman is plain enough: he wouldn't be out there doin' what he's plannin' and doin' it gun naked. That ain't the Tom Huckerman I know.'

'Well, mebbe yuh just don't know him that well no more,' grinned Ed. 'Fellas change.'

'This one don't,' said Coyne as he strolled to the sunlit street. 'This one never has.'

★ ★ ★

It was late into a night still heavy with the heat of day when Sheriff Woods finally got to easing his tired feet from sweat-sticky boots, throwing them aside and pouring himself a measure of whiskey in the back room of his office.

He was glad now it was over. Glad to see the last of Marshal Coyne, the tall, stiff frame of the fellow, silhouetted against the night sky as he rode clear of Trulso for the Broken Necks. Glad, as he had willingly, but thankfully, put it to have 'been of service'; to Curtis for looking to the Marshal's horse, organizing food, a hot bath and rest for the fellow, and more than glad that the one-time lawman had said nothing

69

around town of who he was, why he was here and where he was heading.

Nobody, Ed had figured, needed to know. Trulso's Tom Huckerman was not for being destroyed by no hearsay talk of a gunslinging past.

Not, he had also figured, that Huckerman's past was all hearsay, not if a fellow of the likes of Marshal Coyne could devote his retirement to tracking him and do it well enough to get this far — to back-of-beyond and nowhere Trulso. Nossir! That was dedication, and maybe a whole lot more.

So, sure, he was glad to see the back of the fellow. Trouble was, he had left behind a lingering doubt in Sheriff Woods's mind that was going to plague like bed-ticks through a hot, sleepless night.

Supposing — *just* supposing — Marshal Coyne was not retired. He had said he was, but who was to know for certain? And supposing he was not Frank Coyne's brother at all? What if he was some other marshal all for closing the book on Tom Huckerman; some lawman with a real grudge against a fellow whose shadow he had trailed for years?

Supposing the marshal he had sent out there to the Broken Necks was for killing Tom Huckerman minute he clapped eyes on him?

Or was that 'supposing' a mite too far?

It had been a long, hot day, not the sort he had planned.

What he should have done was ask for proof of that damned marshal's identity . . .

Hell, that is exactly what he should have done!

It took Sheriff Woods just fifteen minutes then to pull on his boots, buckle his gunbelt, tack a scribbled note to the door of his office, collect a Winchester from the cabinet, saddle his horse and be riding clear of Trulso, due north into the Broken Necks.

'Where else?' he had grunted, slapping the mount to a gallop.

8

Dori Maguire had been having her own identity problem for most of that second morning of trailing behind Tom Huckerman into the eerie loneliness of the mountain range.

First day's tracking from the creek stream had passed quiet enough, without a second thought for the fate of Mohawk Stein, and the concentration settled on how best and how long it might take to reach whatever remained of the place called Morton.

Tom had opted for staying with the only visible track. 'T'ain't a deal,' he had said as they joined it at sun-up, 'but while ever it's headin' north it'll do. Best we got, anyhow.'

All they had got, Dori had reckoned through the long, hot hours of moving ever deeper into the silence and hugging shadows of the Broken Necks, but for the man up ahead of her it was another sliver of hope, a chance that the raiders holding his daughter were doing precisely what men of their kind and thinking usually did: went deep, stayed low, let the heat cool and figured the next move.

Even so, that young gal would fast become a burden, needing to be fed, watered and looked to, hardly the regular chore scumbag roughnecks would welcome. Sooner or later one of them would get to being the barrel's bad apple.

And maybe it was that, the thought of time closing in like a night for the girl, that was keeping Tom Huckerman preoccupied with the crucifix he turned constantly through his fingers, one eye never seeming to leave it, when he should have been scanning the trail.

When he might, along with Dori, have wondered just who it was following them . . .

First hint of being watched had come at dawn that morning as Dori was loading the trail mount. Not a deal to it, just the softest slip of a shadow among the higher rocks, but at a time when shadows were not for shifting. Trick of the fingering light; something a tensed body and mind on a knife-edge could imagine without even trying? Could be, Dori had thought. One thing was for sure, it had escaped Tom Huckerman's notice. Or maybe it was all second nature to a one-time gunslinger to never react to anything, real or imagined, till you were good and ready.

He was still not reacting four hours later; still just sitting his mount, letting the crucifix drift like trapped light through his fingers, when somewhere up there, Dori was certain now, somebody was still watching and following close as he could get, or dared.

Or was she plain spooked?

Heck, just who in his right mind would want to trail the Broken Necks anyhow? Nobody got this deep without good reason — those on the run or those running to catch them — and nobody held to following just out of gunshot range without making it clear it was the destination, not the trailing, that intrigued.

So, just who . . . ?

Hold it, the man had pocketed the crucifix, was reining back, slowing the pace.

'Don't suppose it's escaped yuh notice — ' he began softly.

'No, it ain't!' snapped Dori. 'And yuh might've said it hadn't yours, damn yuh! I been — '

'Reckoned so,' said Tom through a tight grin. 'Well, he ain't gettin' closer, so he ain't for haltin' us in a hurry. Just watchin' and followin'. Question: where'd he spring from and where does he figure we're headin'?'

'Must've been holed-up hereabouts since sundown,' said Dori, glancing quickly to the rocks. 'But, hell, he can't know what we're about, can he? Not no how.'

'Not unless he knows there's only Morton up ahead and figures us for goin' there.'

'One of them raiders?'

Tom shrugged and eased the sweat at his hatband. 'Could be. One of the scum posted look-out. Could've heard the shootin' at the creek.'

'Could've seen that crucifix yuh been twirlin' since sun-up,' pouted Dori, a deal sharper than she intended.

'He was meant to,' murmured Tom.

'Yuh mean — '

'If he is one of the scum, he's got a choice, ain't he? Must've recognized me for the fella back there at Trulso, so he can either let us go on 'til we're into the rats' nest, or take us in about — ' Tom glanced at the climbing sun — ''bout an hour from now, soon as he's into shadow and this track's like a furnace. Give him the edge, won't it?'

'That's gunslinger's talk,' quipped Dori.

'Gunslinger's *thinking*!' grinned Tom.

'And it don't worry yuh none, him waitin' on the sun and us waitin' on hot lead?'

'Not right now it don't,' said Tom, slipping his fingers to his pocket for the crucifix. 'Fella's figurin' it for bein' easy, ain't he? Reckons me for bein' a pa in distress, all lathered up over the loss of his gal, and you for bein' what yuh are — a woman. Mebbe he'll spare yuh for later.'

'The hell he will!' huffed Dori. 'If he's reckonin' — '

'So we just move on, yuh hear? Real steady. No hurry. And no glancin' his way. But when I say shift, the hell, ma'am, yuh shift!'

'And then?' asked Dori, beginning to sweat.

'Then I'll kill the sonofabitch,' said Tom, easing his mount forward.

★ ★ ★

Dori Maguire spent most of the next hour watching the shadows as if they

77

were killer mountain lions all set to lunge to the track with only one thing in mind.

Damn it, she had thought through sudden spasms of shivering and shaking, she had passed two-thirds of her life waiting on men lathering up to show their worst, but straight out, cold-blooded killing had not on those occasions been uppermost in their reckoning. Most they had wanted then was to get their grubby paws on her, and that, for all the disgust it had raised in her, she could handle.

This was a whole lot different. This was going to be no-frills, no-quarter murder.

And Tom Huckerman was right — the fellow up there, skulking through the rocks like a thirsty sand bug sniffing out water, would strike the minute he figured the odds were all with him. But was Huckerman right to hold to the track like he was; why not get clear of it now, sneak into cover, force the raider to show himself, wear his patience till he was too tired and sun-fazed to focus, when he might just get careless?

Seemed like good sense in Dori's figuring. Only way in her book to handle a fellow intent on making a grab was to stay out of reach. Tom Huckerman's way was to take the fellow's hand!

But, then, she had reasoned, Tom Huckerman was, or had been, a gunslinger, and men of that calling had minds of their own. No arguing, no compromise, not if you wanted to stay with their guns on your side. Simple fact. And right now, the simple fact was that Huckerman was holding to the track, just idling away there, his mount at a slow, even pace, as if reckoning on there being all the time in the world to get wherever he was heading.

But she would give a whole lot to see the look in his eyes, to be levelling with his thoughts, to know just how many times he had been here before, on a track among mountains with a killer walking in his steps . . .

Another shiver, like cold fingers tapping on her bones, broke Dori's musing as her gaze sharpened on Tom's back. He had stiffened, pocketed the crucifix, settled both hands easy but not loose on the reins. She glanced quickly at the deepening shadows among the high rocks. Sun was swinging round, darkening over the fellow up there, glaring like a fierce eye on the track down here.

Maybe now was the time. Maybe Huckerman had seen something, heard something, or maybe it was just a gunslinger's sixth sense, the instinct that gave him the edge.

She had no more time to figure it as the man half-turned in the saddle with a suddenness that made Dori jerk, flashed her a piercing glance, mouthed something inaudible and in the next moment had swung his mount clear of the track and into a sprawling heap of boulders.

Dori followed, dragging the trail mount back of her, rolling to the pitch of her own mount's slithering through loose rock, not daring to look back but with her eyes still wild and wide as she slewed to a halt at the side of Tom's horse and realized, with a deeper, colder shiver behind her sweat, that horses were all the company she would be sharing from here on.

Tom Huckerman had disappeared.

9

Wait, hold your breath, listen, watch for that first shift of the light. Let the silence do the talking. Just like the old times.

Tom hugged the shadows in the space between the boulders, heard Dori Maguire slither into hiding from the track, licked his lips and lifted his gaze to the sprawling mass of rock above him.

Not a sound and nothing moving. It figured, he thought, blinking on a surge of sweat. Fellow would be weighing the odds right now, reckoning on his prey burying themselves clear of the track and settling to sit it out.

He would not be figuring for himself being the hunted.

Tom slid a hand to the rock face, eased his weight to it, then moved like an inching caterpillar a few feet higher.

'Easy, easy,' he murmured through a hiss of breath, there was no hurry, not yet, not while ever the fellow stayed with his figuring and waiting. He would want to be sure before he made a positive move.

Human nature.

Tom waited again, this time fixing his gaze on the spread of rock ahead of him. No difficulty in moving on, he decided. He could ease his way forward to where the boulders petered out and the tumbling slabs of rock from the higher reaches hung in a jawline of ledges and overhangs. And once there, with any one of a half-dozen niches and clefts for cover, he would have a clear view of an approach from any direction.

He cursed at the snort of one of the mounts behind him, and shifted his weight.

Stalking fellow up there would be reckoning on doing the same. He had waited long enough. Time had come to make his move, slip lower through the shadows to where the mounts were hitched, then find himself a suitable cleft, plenty of cover, deep shade, nicely placed for the measured rifle shot. And before the skulking folk down there knew what had hit them . . .

It would be over, thought Tom, creeping on to the nearest ledge, in a few, fast shots. Somebody would get over anxious, careless, take one step too many, grab for the rock that was just out of reach, relax the concentration, shift the steady gaze, lather up a mite too much confidence.

Human nature.

He paused within a few steps of the ledge, a frown creasing his brow. Might be smarter to keep this fellow alive, find out exactly where his partners were holed up, beat every last dreg of what he could tell of Holly from him until there was nothing.

He swallowed on his retching anger, blinked the images clear and came back to focusing on the rocks. Hell, that had been the moment when he might have got careless, when instead of watching he had been wandering.

He winced at another snort from the mounts. Damn it, had the woman no notion of how to keep a mount silent? Might have been a whole lot simpler leaving her to silence some loud-mouthed bull of a drunkard. She would have handled him! As it was, she was guiding the stalker to her faster than attracting flies to dead meat.

'Shift!' he hissed to himself and slid a boot to the next safe foothold.

Not so safe. Nothing like!

He watched the loose stone he had dislodged trundle its slow way down the narrow slope between the boulders, a flurry of pebbles in its wake.

Hold it.

Wait.

Listen.

He had only seconds then before the shadow spread like black wings across the ledge ahead of him; barely time to swallow on the sharp intake of breath before he heard the slithering scrape of boots, saw the shape of a leg, a body and the glinting, probing thrust of a barrel levelled true and steady at his guts.

'Now ain't that just made me a dandy day!' drawled the man through a sneering grin as he steadied himself on the ledge and glared at Tom. 'My, was that a fool thing to go doin', and just when I was figurin' yuh for havin' an edge there.'

Tom's eyes narrowed and tightened on the fellow's face. Last time he had seen it had been through a cloud of swirling smoke; a wind-chafed, pitted face, with staring eyes and a slant to the lips over cracked, broken teeth. A face that seemed now, as then, in the chaos and misery of the burning homestead, to be on fire. A face from the haunting images on the high plain out of Trulso.

'Reckoned yuh for dead, fella,' sneered the man again, with a twitchy thrust of the barrel. 'Should've been cooked in that flamin' hell-hole we left.'

Tom's eyes stayed narrowed, unblinking, one hand spread to the rock face, the other loose as a leaf at his side. 'Wrong,' he croaked.

'Well, we ain't for havin' yuh around, yuh hear — specially not no tear-jerkin' pa of that gal we sprung from yuh.'

Tom flinched on a sudden bubbling of his blood, a swimming burst of sweat, an almost uncontrollable urge to reach for a Colt and blast that fiery, slant-lipped face into oblivion. All it needed was the speed of the old days, the same, steady glare that read a man, the flash of fingers . . . same as it had been on the morning he had taken out Vince Ristoff with just one shot.

'Ain't for sayin' a deal, are yuh, fella,' grinned the man. 'Holdin' to yuh thoughts there, eh? Well, I ain't for interruptin' yuh. Make this quick, shall I, so's I can get to that woman yuh trailin' along of yuh?' The grin slanted deep into the corner of his mouth. 'And don't yuh fret none — I'll give yuh regards to yuh gal next time I get to fondlin' her!'

Tom Huckerman might then have

lost his reasoning, might have seen nothing save the shape of the man, the sheer, leering bulk of him, and thrown himself into a frenzy of attack.

And been dead, he still had the sense to reckon, the few seconds it would take for the man to squeeze the trigger and the rifle to blaze its fury.

He stayed steady, near motionless, his stare locked into the man's eyes as if boring through them, hands easy, fingers lifeless — only the tip of his boot beginning to move.

If there had been one loose stone, there had to be another . . .

'Oh, my, oh, my, ain't you the picture there of the lost soul waitin' on his Maker!' The man's grin spread to a mocking smile. 'Gotta hand it to yuh, though — '

He handed out nothing, not another sneer, not another word, and barely another gesture, as the shift of no more than a pebble to the slope and its chattering slide over rock broke his concentration for the split-second it needed for Tom's Colt to be drawn and raging freely from the knuckle-white grip at his hip.

The man groaned, doubled, spat a mouthful of blood, lost his hold on the rifle and sank slowly, like a body on melting grease legs, to the ground.

Tom waited, watching, the sweat cold and gleaming on his face, one hand tight on the smoking Colt, the other drifting almost casually to its twin. Only when the pair were drawn and levelled did he crunch the few steps forward to stand over the man and release the blaze from both barrels into his face until what had once been fiery became an inferno.

'Human nature,' he murmured, staring at the devastation, ' 'cepting yuh weren't no part of it.'

★　★　★

It was a full five minutes before Dori Maguire had stumbled her way through the boulders to Tom's side. 'Hell,' she croaked, staring at the body, 'ain't that just . . . '

She gulped, caught her breath, stood back, stifled a retch and ran her fingers over her eyes.

'I heard what the fella said,' she murmured, reaching to lay a hand on Tom's shoulder but thinking better of it. 'Almost certain them scum are holed up at Morton. Gotta be. And it can't be far on. Mebbe we could be there come sun-up t'morrow.'

'T'night,' said Tom, turning to face her. 'We'll be there t'night.'

'Well, I ain't so certain about that, mister. I mean, we gotta eat, rest up a while, and them mounts — '

'T'night,' snapped Tom, swinging his gaze to the meandering twists of the track. 'We move on now. No restin' up'.

'Now hold on there, fella, yuh seem to be over-lookin' somethin' here. I ain't exactly in one whole piece m'self — 'case yuh f'gotten — and I ain't exactly used to spendin' every few hours standin' in to a shootin'! Hell, mister, bodies are pilin' up like — '

'Yuh ridin' or plannin' on settin' up home?' asked Tom. 'Choice is yours.'

Dori Maguire said nothing as she watched the man head back to the mounts.

10

Sheriff Ed Woods had made a choice which right now, as he struggled to hold his tired mount on the track to the dry-bed creek, was beginning to look increasingly like the wrong one.

Hell, he thought, flicking a lather of sweat from his cheeks, supposing he had got this all wrong and was chasing a lame steer round its own corral. He had nothing, not a snitch, to raise any real doubts in his mind about the motives or the identity of the retired Marshal Coyne, and, in truth, was maybe meddling in a pot he had no claim to.

Tom Huckerman's past was Tom's affair to be either lived with or settled as he saw fit.

What had happened out there at the fellow's homestead on the plain, was another matter. That *was* a sight more than Tom's affair, that involved the self-respect, sense of justice and decency of every man, and none should shirk it, least of all himself.

But he had, damn it! Should never have let Tom leave like that; should have done more to persuade him against it, or failing that, ridden with him.

On the other hand, if Tom Huckerman was who Marshal Coyne said he was, or had been, then the hard-riding, hard-living, gunslinging Huckerman was a man more than able to look to himself. No small-time lawman was ever going to be more than somebody loading the fellow's guns when it came, if it came, to a showdown with the scum he was hounding.

Even so, somebody had to load the guns.

So, was that the top and tail of his being out here — to load Tom Huckerman's guns? Well, maybe it was at that, and maybe against all-comers, including retired marshals with or without a chip on their shoulder.

In the meantime . . . The creek was dry, the day getting hotter, the mount as worn as old leather, and the track ahead, deep into the Broken Necks, looking meaner by the hour.

But there was that faint finger of grey smoke out there, a deal further to the east than he would have preferred, but maybe somebody to share a bite with. Who knows, might even be Marshal Coyne!

★   ★   ★

It was a sprawling heap of old timbers, dust and dirt-smeared windows, warped door, turf roof and pipe chimney, leaning veranda, patched and mended at random and dumped at the far end of a dry, narrow creek like a lifetime of trash. If the Devil had some place he rested up, Brenard's was it. And you could bet your sweet life that what you saw on the outside was a mirror image of what you would find in the stale, drink-drenched gloom beyond the open door, thought Ed, reining up where the track petered out to a dust bowl.

He grunted and sat easy, his gaze moving slowly from left to right. Handful of hitched, mangy mounts, collection of barrels, pails, chewed besoms, pair of old boots, one-time wagon — crippled on two wheels — scattering of empty bottles and, groaning under the weight of wet blankets and a limp, lifeless bar-girl's dress, a washing-line.

No sign of anything that might pass for life and nothing as yet disturbing the silence. Sleeping it off, thought Ed, or dead of the plague.

He was easing the mount a few steps closer when a body, smothered in a ragged blanket of stitched sacks, was thrown from the dark interior to the shaded veranda.

Ed drew the mount to a sharp halt and peered closer. Naked leg, naked arm, what might pass for a head of hair, a pinched, fear-ridden face behind a mask of dirt, and eyes that watched him as if transfixed by a rattler.

He slid from the saddle, patted the mount's neck and crossed slowly, step by carefully measured step, to the mound of rags. Woman, sure enough, he reckoned, watching the face, or what passed for one hereabouts; half-crazed, near out of her mind, the cracked lips muttering and simpering over sounds that never got to being words, and then, as he came closer, scuttling and squirming like a threatened insect to a cringing ball in the darkest corner.

Ed had a foot on the veranda when the door space was filled by a fat, gut-rolling man chewing hungrily on a cigar slanting from the side of his wide mouth.

'Ain't worth a spit right now,' he drawled, releasing a cloud of smoke across his sidelong glance at the woman. 'Give her an hour, she'll come round.' He fingered the cigar from his mouth and fixed his gaze on the sheriff. 'Come far?' he asked, the woman dismissed.

'South,' murmured Ed, still watching the mound of rags. 'She don't look — ' he began again.

'Don't concern y'self, mister. They get to bein' like that this time of day.' The man spat towards the corner. 'Lazy bitch.' He grunted, clamped the cigar between his teeth again and slid his hands to his pockets. 'Name's Brenard. Place here is mine. Food, liquor, girls, gamin', any order of yuh preference, few sideliners come extra. Don't ask no awkward questions, don't expect none. Yuh just passin' through or stayin' awhile?'

Ed drew his gaze reluctantly from the simpering woman. 'Passin' through,' he mumbled, wiping a hand over his sticky face. 'Headin' north. Well, mebbe, mebbe not.'

Brenard's eyes tightened to dark slits. 'Yuh ain't certain?' he croaked.

'Not yet.' Ed shrugged against the

clinging sweat at his shirt. 'Lookin' for a fella.'

'Most are,' grinned the man. 'Lookin' for one, or runnin' from one. Don't matter a damn to me.'

'Old friend of mine. Yuh might know him.'

'If he's a low-life scumbag, two-bit gunslinger, murderin' hound, drunk, or fancy womanizer who fancied once too far, I'll know him. Most been here one time. Not that I'm given to sayin'. T'ain't good for business. Customers don't go much on loose lips.'

'Coyne,' said Ed sharply, 'Fella's name is Coyne. Might've passed this way — '

'Scaffs Coyne,' grunted Brenard through another cloud of smoke. 'Brother to Frank. One-time marshal, law-swinger — 'til the maggots got to him and he changed sides. Penned for ten years for armed robbery out Montana way. Came out a year or so back. That the fella?'

'That's him,' said Ed on a long, dry swallow.

'I know him,' mumbled Brenard, removing the cigar to examine its glowing tip. 'Seen him recently, few hours back. Watered up here and rode on.'

'Well, now,' smiled Ed, 'seems like I got lucky.'

'Don't bank on it, mister. Not yet I wouldn't.'

'How come?' asked Ed on another dry swallow.

Brenard blew softly over the cigar's flickering glow. 'Way I see it, mister, you ride outa here on Scaffs Coyne's trail and I could be settin' a hound on his tail. Who's to say yuh ain't for huntin' him down? Mebbe you and him got some reckonin' to finish.' He paused and raised his dark gaze to Ed's face. 'Who's to say yuh ain't the law?'

'Me?' blustered Ed through a bubbling of cold sweat. 'Me — the law, f'Crissake! Hell, I'm about as way outa the law as yuh can get. Me and Scaffs, why, we go back more years than seems like we been livin'.' He swallowed again, wiped at the sweat, but held Brenard's gaze as if clinging to it like a drowning man, his mind reeling with the effort of lying. 'If he were here right now — '

'Gotta be real careful in my line of business, mister,' drawled Brenard, drawing on the cigar. 'Let a fella down, double deal him a rough edge, and he can get to bein' real nasty. Could put me outa business, yuh understand. So yuh see my problem, don't yuh? I gotta be real certain — '

He turned sharply at the crash of a table somewhere in the depths of the tumbledown building, flung the cigar to the veranda, heeled it and stood back as a half-dressed, half-drunk fellow stumbled to the light, one hand clutching an empty bottle, the other gripping the swathe of bloodstained rags at his shoulder.

'What the hell, Mohawk,' groaned Brenard, steadying the man against the door jamb. 'One more bottle of that stuff and we'll be pouring the dregs on your coffin!'

Ed glanced hurriedly to where his mount waited, then at the cringing woman. Hell, he needed to get clear while he still had the chance, before Brenard got to asking more questions and wasting more time. He had what he wanted, he knew the true identity of Marshal Coyne, knew he must still be heading north and just why.

'Now here's a fine example of what happens when a fella gets to probin' deeper than's good for him,' scoffed Brenard, watching Mohawk Stein sink to his knees at his feet. 'Mohawk here got to tryin' to snaffle one of my gals from some trail-bustin' drifter boastin' fancy Colts. Fella we ain't none of us set eyes on yet. Ain't none too keen to neither if this is a sample of his handlin'.'

'What fella?' snapped Ed, the sweat suddenly colder in his neck. 'Where'd he see him? When?'

'Hey, now,' said Brenard, the gaze

darkening again, 'yuh sure got a real askin' attitude, ain't yuh, mister? Scaffs Coyne, now whoever it was half-killed old Mohawk . . . What's yuh problem, fella, yuh got a bad dose of nosyin', or might it just be — ?'

'Don't matter none,' said Ed, his Colt suddenly tight and heavy in his hand. 'T'ain't your business, but thanks all the same.'

Brenard simply smiled, relaxed and easy on his bulk, as Ed backed away, the Colt levelled, his gaze tight and anxious, and was still smiling and making to light a fresh cigar when the sheriff finally turned to dash the few steps to his waiting mount.

And sure enough the mount was still waiting, patient as ever, but going nowhere, not now, not for a while, and maybe never, he groaned, as his sweat-blurred gaze took in the two men cradling rifles flanking it.

11

Dori Maguire was all through with protesting. It did no good and got her nowhere. Same went for persuasion. Waste of time and grovelling effort. Best leave the fellow to his own mind. There was nothing, short of avalanche or earthquake — and maybe both in equal measure — going to shift Tom Huckerman from riding straight as an arrow down this Godforsaken track. To whatever and wherever it led. Damn him!

She squirmed against the clinging sweat-damp of the poncho, winced at the ache in her legs, the dull thud of bruising, and fixed her gaze on the back of the man in front of her.

Stubborn, determined and single-minded he might be, but who was to blame him? Fellow could only be thinking now he was within a few miles of finding his daughter and coming face to face with the men who had abducted her.

But just how, she wondered, tightening the line of her lips in the thought, did he plan on taking out the five holed up at Morton? And had he reckoned on those same five already beginning to ponder how it was their companion had not shown up? Could be they had even heard the echoes of the shooting back there.

So if Tom Huckerman figured for one minute he was going to just trail that worn mount of his into the web of the ghost buildings, settle the issue and ride out with his daughter tucked comfortably back of him, he should maybe think again.

And probably had, she sighed, watching now as his gaze began that slow, easy swing from left to right, moving like a light through the gathering late afternoon gloom, probing the shadows, every cleft and crevice of the rocks, from the tumbling pounce of them at the side of the track, to the sweeping reach of them to the higher peaks. Gunslinger's gaze, no mistaking.

She shivered. Place and the man were beginning to spook her. Maybe she should bury her own stubborn pride and try just one more time to level with the fellow.

'T'ain't for me to ask, o'course,' she said, drawing her mount alongside Tom, 'but we goin' to ride into this place like we were invited to a hoe-down?'

'You ain't,' murmured Tom, his gaze still roving.

'Oh,' frowned Dori, 'and just what am I goin' to be doin' and where'm I goin' to be doin' it? Kinda like to know.'

'Way I see it, yuh got two choices.'

'Name 'em. I'm all ears!'

Tom's gaze settled on the woman's face. 'Yuh could turn round right now and get y'self holed up safe some place 'til I got the time to come back for yuh.'

'Assumin' you're in any state to do

that,' quipped Dori.

Tom shrugged. 'Like yuh say, assumin' just that, but I ain't so sour-minded over the prospect.'

Dori squirmed again and tightened her grip on the reins.

'Or,' added Tom, 'yuh can keep goin' along of me 'til I figure it's time for yuh to take the horses into cover and stay with 'em.'

'That it?' asked Dori.

'That's it. Choice is yours.'

'Well, now,' said Dori, stiffening, 'one's much the same as the other, ain't it? Either way I get to bein' alone and waitin' on whatever happens to you, and that, way *I* see it, ain't no choice at all. Fried in the pan or fried in the fire, still fried, ain't it? No, Mr Huckerman, won't do, not one bit. I gotta much better way.'

'Like yuh told me — like yuh been tellin' me for long enough — yuh ain't in no fit state — '

'I ain't, but if we go waitin' 'til I am, we'll be far side of winter. Fact is,

106

mister, yuh goin' to need more than them fancy Colts when we head-on to them scum. Yuh goin' to need me with Stotts's Winchester. And don't go thinkin' I can't use it. Watch me!'

'Ma'am, I ain't never had a woman — ' began Tom.

'Yeah, yeah,' drawled Dori, 'I know. Yuh ain't never had a woman along of yuh when it came to a shootin'. Well, that's just fine, 'cus it means yuh can't make a judgement either way, don't it?' She flashed the man a honed glance. 'Yuh figure?' she smiled.

'I been bushwhacked!' croaked Tom.

'That yuh have! And in case yuh — '

'Hold it!' snapped Tom, flattening a hand on the reins of Dori's mount. 'Yuh smell that?'

'Smell what?' sniffed Dori.

'Horses up ahead.'

'We that close?' whispered Dori. 'Hell, I figured us for bein' — '

'Too much figurin' and yuh get to fryin' for real,' said Tom, as he slid softly from his mount and gestured for Dori to follow.

She was shivering when her feet touched the ground.

★ ★ ★

It took Tom twenty vital minutes to bring the mounts into safe, hidden cover, hitch them tight and make clear what he intended to Dori Maguire.

'Morton can't be more than a spit away,' he had murmured, drawing her into the shadows of the boulders. 'Somewhere far side of that reach out there. Seems like the scum got their horses tied close by, so we move well clear of 'em. Don't want them spooked none. Yuh understand?' Dori had licked her lips and nodded. 'You stay near to me and watch for my signals. Don't move a finger 'til I say so, and when yuh do move yuh make it fast and sure, no matter what. No hesitatin', no lookin' back for me. And don't, f'Crissake, get lathered up with that rifle. Yuh carryin' it to protect y'self, nothin' else. Won't be no shootin' 'til it's necessary, and then I'll be doin' it. Yuh got that?' Dori had nodded again. 'So now we creep outa here soft as ants. Light's good for a half-hour. After that . . . ' Tom had paused, his gaze on the woman's face unblinking. 'Guess we'll find out soon enough.'

'Yuh figure yuh gal for bein' — ' Dori had whispered.

'I don't figure nothin', ma'am. Figurin' gets dangerous.'

So what in hell's name was this, thought Dori, ten minutes later as she struggled through the rocks three steps short of Tom Huckerman's shadow, the easy bit? Fellow drew a fine line this side of danger!

But, then, she mused, reaching for the next hand-hold, he had done all this before, you could bet; crept through the gathering dark, the twilight between sundown and moon up, same as an animal might to its supper.

Some supper!

And just supposing, when it was all done and they were still, God willing, alive and breathing, there was no sign of the girl? What if the raiders . . .

She waited, staring at Tom's raised hand, hardly daring to swallow, the sweat trickling in cold streams down her back. What now? Had he seen something, heard something? Damn it, even the shadows were alive, every one of them, like they were bodies on the move, slipping this way, that, straight ahead, back of you, left and right. Any one of them might be . . .

They were moving again.

Slower now, softer; feathers caught in the draught of a breeze; Tom slipping quickly, silently, from rock to rock as if crossing a river on stepping-stones.

Dori swallowed, this time wincing on the parched bite of the dryness, eased her shoulders against the cling of the poncho and weight of the rifle, and crept on, following instinctively in Tom's footholds. Still nothing to see save the bulging shadows, shifting fast into night now on the fading light, the scrawled line of rocks, mounds of boulders and the dark twisted crevices between them. But nothing of the shapes of Morton, nothing of the mounts Tom had smelled, not a hint, in fact, that there had been life in these parts since the one-time settlement had flourished.

She shivered again. No life, but you could sure as hell sense the ghosts!

A raised hand, another pause. Silence. The hand gestured for Dori to come on to Tom's side. She gulped and scrambled like a threatened insect into his shadow.

It seemed an age to Dori before Tom finally lifted himself a fraction higher in the rocks to peer over them and then, with a hand on her shoulder, draw her to his level.

'One horse,' he murmured, nodding to where the single mount stood loose-hitched, sad-eyed and sweating at the foot of a rocky slope. 'Must've heard the shootin' back there, figured their partner weren't goin' to show and pulled out.'

'The scumbags have gone?' hissed Dori.

'Like the wind,' grunted Tom.

'But left the fella's horse. Why?'

'Wanted whoever was followin' to find it,' said Tom, easing to his full height.

'Don't figure it,' frowned Dori, standing up to squirm and flex her shoulders beneath the poncho. 'Don't make sense.'

'Old trick, seen it before,' said Tom, swinging his gaze over the spread of shadows and looming dark. 'Kinda warning, just to let us know they got our measure and one eye waitin' on us followin'.'

'So what now?' frowned Dori again.

'So we go see what else they left,' croaked Tom, moving out of the rocks to the slope. 'Horses won't be the only thing, yuh can bet on that.'

Dori was back to shivering.

★ ★ ★

They passed from the rocks to a lower, dustier level of loose stones and the scraps of long-dead trees and brush; a place where the heat of day was gathered as if in a cauldron, where the night seemed deeper and darker and straining like a prisoner at the reach of sheer rock to the higher peaks where, too, the ghosts of Morton lay in a creaking tumble of leaning, leering shapes.

Parts of the buildings of the settlement were still standing: old, misshapen walls, doors on a single, squeaking hinge, windows blank and black as empty eye-sockets, the splintered bones of a boardwalk, fingers of dead rafters where wind and rain had scalped a roof, the sticks of broken chairs and tables, shards of shattered glass, rusted cans, a bald brush head, disintegrating besom, and the smell, thought Dori, walking carefully at Tom's side down what had once been a main street, of decay, something dying but not quite dead.

She shuffled into the man's steady pace, glancing quickly at his levelled gaze, the slow drift of the eyes from left to right, ahead to the creaking wall of darkness, and once, without warning, backwards as if disturbed by a following step.

Nothing, save the sounds of somewhere long deserted.

'Ain't a livin' soul here,' she whispered. 'They must've pulled out hours back.' She huddled into the cold damp of the poncho and shuddered. 'Mebbe we should — '

Tom had halted, his right hand settling like a moth on the butt of a Colt, his gaze tight and sharp now on the dark bulk of the shape ahead.

Some sort of single-storey store, space where doors and windows should have been, but a roof intact and, to the left, a hitching rail, mounds of horse dung beneath it.

'They holed up right there,' murmured Tom, moving on, the Colt drawn, his steps suddenly sharper, slower.

He reached the slanting remains of frontage boardwalk, Dori close in on his steps, paused a moment, watched, listened, grunted and went on, each footfall measured and weighed.

Trash and mess and the stench of unwashed men, thought Dori, sniffing and stifling a sneeze. Sure, the scumbags had been here and left their marks like animals, but now there was only the darkness, the aching joints of rotting timbers where the night breeze found a weakness.

Tom's thumbnail flicked a match into life.

Dori blinked behind the flare. Shadows, a tumbling mass of them over crates, boxes, a one-time bar or counter, a cracked, cobwebbed mirror hanging like a half-closed eye, scuffed dirt and dust across floorboards.

The glow hovered and went out. Tom

flicked at another match, this time lifting it higher to sway the glow over the far end of the store. He was rigidly still for a moment, hardly breathing, the match flame flaring and creeping to the tips of his fingers, his gaze frozen on the sight before him.

A girl's dress, dirt-streaked, torn and bloodstained had been fastened to a rafter like some sodden rag hung out to dry.

'In God's name!' croaked Dori, a sudden sweat oozing to the poncho as she watched Tom flick a third match into life and take the few steps to stand under the rafter.

It was a full ten seconds then before he holstered the Colt and raised his hand to the dress to touch it lightly, gently, as if expecting to feel some movement beneath the fabric, and the flare was almost spent when he murmured 'Holly', and finally closed his fingers in a vicious, angry grip that would rip the dress free of the timber.

Dori's mouth was open on words that

cringed to a scream as the rafter cracked and moaned and spewed a cloud of ancient dust.

'Let go! F'Crissake, let go! It's a trap,' she yelled, but to nothing more than the splintering grind and snap of the timbers as the rafter collapsed bringing with it a crashing mass of planks and joists.

There was no more than a crumpled corner of the dress to be seen when Dori was able to crawl through the debris to where Tom Huckerman had been standing.

12

Sheriff Ed Woods inched his way through the pitch darkness of the shack to the faint chink of light between the timbers of the door, stooped to it, closed one eye and squinted into the moonlit space beyond.

Dirt, rocks, a tethered mount, night.

Same as he had seen last time he looked. Same as he would go on seeing, damn it, for just as long as that sonofabitch Brenard decided to keep him penned like a dog.

'Hell!' he cursed and stood upright, blinking on the darkness, sniffing against the stench of the shack. He turned, thrust his hands to the pockets of his pants and closed his eyes.

Think, man, think!

Brenard was suspicious, reckoning Ed for either a lawman or some scavenging bounty hunter counting the dollars on Scaffs Coyne's head. Whichever, Ed was going nowhere in Brenard's book till he had some answers, and maybe not then, not once the owner of this two-bits spread got to rummaging in Ed's saddle-bags and discovered his badge.

Maybe he already had. Maybe it was only a matter of time now before one of Brenard's whiskey-loused sidekicks opened the door at Ed's back and filled the shack full of hot lead.

So what was keeping him!

He wiped a hot, sticky hand over his face and blinked again on the darkness.

What of Tom Huckerman, he wondered? If that fellow Mohawk's account of 'fancy Colts' was to be believed, then maybe that had been Huckerman making his way north. But what, he also wondered, of the one-time Marshal Coyne? He would have made fast miles since leaving Trulso, maybe to come within spitting distance of Tom. Too late now to reckon on catching up with either of them, but if Tom stayed breathing he was still going to need all the help he could summon against the homestead raiders. If, on the other hand, Coyne got lucky and took his revenge, then Ed would have only one mission open to him — to square things for Tom Huckerman.

Sure, he thought, that clear-cut! Only thing stopping him were the four walls of this darned shack.

Ed turned back to the door and ran his fingers over it. Tight as a new shoe to a hoof. No hope of breaking through it. He moved on, his hands flat to the walls, sensing for the slightest weakness, the one loose plank that might shift under pressure. No luck, not this side. He paused, peering round him. No windows. Roof looked solid. What about the back wall, he wondered, shuffling over the floorboards.

His hands and fingers sensed again, probing, smoothing, touching, pressing on the softest creak, listening for the slightest squeak. Nothing, damn it! Place was as tight as a stone-built jail.

He stepped back, tempted for one crazy moment to thud a boot into the timbers, raise hell and get the whole mess over, and stood without daring to move when his heels sank on a weakened floorboard.

He stayed exactly where he was for a full minute, fearful that in moving he might lose the spot, wondering if just a mite of pressure might sink the board to the earth below it.

Could he get that lucky? Damn it, did he have the time to ponder?

Seconds later he was on his knees, his fingers scrambling for the gaps between the boards, easing into the widest, gripping, lifting until what he now figured for being a whole area of rotting planks was on the move.

Only a matter of keeping his head now, he reckoned, working quickly but quietly to clear a space just wide enough for him to squeeze through.

He sweated, swallowed on his grunts, winced at the grazed soreness across his fingers, felt a trickle of blood over his knuckles, but worked on. With three boards lifted, he paused, peered into the gap, dropped a hand to the dirt below and began the slow process of squeezing and squirming his way to freedom.

Sure, he thought, he *could* get that lucky. But for how long?

★   ★   ★

He was slithering like a hunting rattler, his body flat to the still warm earth, his eyes wide and wet and probing, hands flat and then the fingers hooked to claws as he inched steadily, slowly to the edge of the space beneath the shack.

He paused, conscious of the sweat dripping from his chin, plastering his shirt to his back, stinging in his groin, and narrowed his gaze on what he could see. Not a deal from this angle: vague outline of Brenard's place, shadowed in the blur of lantern light, the legs of his mount hitched to the right, trash, pile of logs, boulders and the pitch-dark depths of the night among the Broken Necks.

But no bodies. Not so much as a stray boot.

So maybe however many holed up with Brenard were all otherwise engaged, supping on the cheap booze, trapped in a fixed game of cards, seeking the cold pleasures of the sad-eyed girls. Well, stay that way, he thought. But how long before Brenard sent a sidekick to check on him? Hell, door there in the shadows of the veranda might open any minute and one of them rifle-cradling louse step out and head this way.

No chance for him then, not like this, armed to the teeth with bare hands!

He swallowed, slithered another foot, paused again and set to reckoning just how far to the mount and the time it would take to reach it, mount up and ride clear. Minutes, he thought, only minutes. But it took less than a minute to die.

He blinked. Longer he stayed where he was, the worse it got. Nothing else for it, time to shift, fast, low and silent, no pausing for glances, just keep your eyes, Ed Woods, on that mount, and stay easy when you reach it. If the horse gets to being spooked . . .

What the hell — blaze of light on the veranda as the door opened; shouted curse, a thud, croaked scream, another curse, crack of a bull-whip, and then the simpering girl in the mound of rags was scrambling through the dirt, the swishing bite of the whip driving her on like she was some straying heifer.

'Damn!' hissed Ed, backing the few inches from the edge of the space as the girl scrambled to her feet, stumbled, ran a few, tottering paces and collapsed again.

He flicked his gaze to the man with the whip. If he decided to come on, if his lathered up, booze-sodden anger was not yet done . . . No, he was still now, the whip loose at his side, legs straddled, face wet and gleaming with sweat. 'What the hell,' he croaked, and spat, then turned and ambled back on to the veranda, his mutterings rumbling through him like a slide of rocks.

Ed released a head of tight breath, blinked, flattened his hands to the earth and stared at the girl. She was near to being all through, he thought, watching the nerve-shattered twitches through her body, the jerky twists in her limbs. Damn it, she needed somebody . . .

No, not him! No chance, there was no time, not if he was going to get to the horse, get clear and back to where he should be, on the trail of Coyne and coming to Tom Huckerman's side.

But, hell, how could he . . . ?

He squirmed to the edge of the space again. All quiet now, save for the simpering girl. Door was closed. Light back to being soft and blurred. The night almost empty.

Shift!

Ed was on his feet, bent low and moving quickly to the mount, when the girl struggled to her knees and hissed across the dark, 'North. He went north. Fella yuh lookin' for. He'll head for Morton.'

Ed stopped, staring, a dry tongue licking over parched lips. 'Thanks,' he murmured, and was set to move again when, almost without realizing it, he had reached for the girl with an outstretched arm and croaked, 'Show me the way. Yuh can do that?'

The girl nodded as she scrambled to his side and took his hand, the softest hint of a smile flickering across her bruised, dirt-smudged face. 'Yuh goin' to need this,' she said, handing him a Colt from beneath the mound of rags.

★   ★   ★

It was a full ten minutes later, with Ed and the girl already deep into the night and the peaks of the Broken Necks ahead of them, when the door to the veranda opened again and Brenard, flanked by two sidekicks, strolled into the pool of light and eased a long, curling twist of cigar smoke across the darkness.

'Yuh know what to do,' he grunted without looking at the men. 'I want 'em dead, every last one. Take whatever's worth the trouble, but don't leave nothin' breathin' — man or woman.'

13

Start again, take your time, think it through and go easy on the panic. Nothing to be gained if you panic. Damn it, you might just end up killing the fellow!

Dori Maguire drew the poncho slowly over her head, threw it aside, flicked the stragglings of her hair into her neck and slid gently to her knees, her eyes round and bright but piercing like beams at the tangle before her.

She spat into her hands, rubbed them together and took a deep breath. This was probably going to be beyond her, way out of her strength, but, hell, she had to try, just had to do something before Tom Huckerman breathed his last.

'Get to it, f'Crissake!' she hissed, blinking furiously for a clearer sight against the gloom and still drifting dust. 'Just do it!'

Her hands settled on the bulk of the rafter pinning Tom to the ground in a mound of splintered timbers. She glanced quickly into his face. Eyes were still closed, trickles of blood from his temple and the cuts and grazes across his cheeks, but he was breathing — oh, yes, he was breathing, sure enough, laboured and sometimes through a choking gurgle, but alive, and if she could just manage . . .

She gasped as she heaved against the bulk, sweated until the lather shone like beads across her flesh, tried to lift, then to push, her full weight pressed against the rafter.

'Shift, damn yuh!' she croaked.

Tom groaned, the timbers creaked, a drift of dust shimmered to the shafts of moonlight through the open roof, but nothing moved. Dori slumped back and ran a hand over her face, into her neck and breasts, grimacing at the sudden chill of the sweat, then licking her lips and staring again at the near lifeless body of Tom Huckerman.

Hell, she thought, he really was going to die, right there, under the bulk of the rafter, his fingers still clutching his daughter's dress. And there was not a damn thing she could do about it.

She shivered, hugged herself and struggled back to the rafter. How long, she wondered, before the man stopped breathing? Another hour, another day? Maybe she should do the decent thing — grab the Winchester and put the fellow out of his misery. The hell she would!

So maybe she should go for help. But from where — Brenard's? Sonofabitch would never get to lifting a finger for nobody, specially one half dead. Put a bullet between his eyes and strip him clean of anything worth taking more like. Trulso was too far back, and up ahead . . . Nothing, save rock and dirt and sun-baked mountains, not to mention the scumbag raiders.

She shivered again. Just what sort of

minds were they that would lay a trap like they had? Damn it, they had known, right through to their bones, that the man would reach for the dress. Only natural, plain instinct, and Tom Huckerman, for all his smart gun-slinger's thinking and figuring, had done no more, no less than any pa. And paid the price along of it.

But had he, even at the moment of touching Holly's dress, been reassured that its hanging there meant the girl was still alive, that the raiders were taking her on to wherever they were destined?

She stared into Tom's grey, blood-streaked face. Sure he had known, she thought, must have. That was why he was still breathing, still hanging in there like some fly with one leg in a web.

Dori wiped the sweat from her shoulders, licked her lips and spat into her hands again. If Tom Huckerman could hang in there for his girl, so could she — only this time she would be praying along of the sweating. Not that the praying had done a deal of good for her in the past. Trail-sour fellows had still had their hands all over just the same, and no amount of prayers had saved her from the likes of Brenard. But when you came to it, in a situation like this, what else was there?

Start again, she thought, with another spit into her hands. Go easy on the panic. And pray, damn it!

* * *

Dori Maguire had been heaving, praying — and cursing! — for nearly another hour and getting nowhere with the fallen rafter save to deepen the groans in Tom Huckerman's throat, when she slumped back again, this time with tears as wet and flowing in her eyes as the sweat across her back.

She was done, all through, washed up and clean out of another bite of strength. Nothing else for it now, she reckoned, she would have to go seek some help, slip into that stinking poncho again, leave the fellow as comfortable as she could make him, hope against hope he stayed breathing and offer herself up to Brenard against the price of him doing something, anything, even if it meant the bullet between the eyes.

But, hell, she was going to live with the grief and anger of it for the rest of her life, and if the time ever came when she might get lucky enough to wreak some revenge on them scumbag raiders.

Only then, in that moment of wiping away another flood of tears, did Dori reckon herself for going mad.

She was already seeing things in the Godforsaken bones of that ghost town: shadows that were suddenly the shapes of men, flickerings of moonlight that seemed like the approach of swinging lanterns, the tangle of splintered timbers coming to life in a cluster of reaching arms and hands.

And now she was hearing things.

The steady scuff of hoofs through loose dirt, the creak of saddle leather, soft, tinkling jangle of tack, the snort of a tired mount. Two ticks to a bedroll she would have sworn that a rider was coming in.

She saw him through the wet blur of her tears, a tall, dark, dust-coated fellow, his eyes as sharp as washed pebbles, just standing there in the ruins of the broken building as if — yeah, thought Dori, blinking, swallowing, running her hands across her cheeks, as if in answer to a prayer.

★ ★ ★

She had no idea who he was, where he had come from, of how in a hundred miles of wild territory in any direction he had stumbled into a place like Morton, or why, and nor did she care in those first minutes of the man staring first at her, his eyes narrowing as he took in the sight of her nakedness from the waist up, and then, a deal more measured and slower, at the body beneath the fallen rafter.

'Can yuh . . . ?' Dori had croaked, and swallowed instantly on her words as the man slid out of the dust-coat, unbuckled his gunbelt, rolled his shirtsleeves and bent to the situation with no more than a grunt.

'I just can't . . . ' she had begun again, struggling into the poncho through another bout of shivering.

'Just lend a hand that far side, ma'am,' the man had murmured, flexing his fingers on his grip on the rafter. 'Lift when I tell yuh. Real easy. No rush.'

'Sure, sure. Anythin' yuh say. I been tryin' — '

'Now!'

Dori winced at the creaking cracks and groans as the timber shifted like the limb of some sprawled giant stirred in sleep.

'Hold it!' grunted the man, the muscles in his arms bulging under the lift, sweat already gleaming on his face. 'Ease yuh end round real slow. Slower . . . then down 'til it's restin'.'

135

'Got it!' moaned Dori.

'Right. Now get to the fella. Take his legs, pull him clear. One fast drag, and don't fret if he screams some. Move!'

Tom Huckerman's body slid from the bulk of the rafter with a scuffed, grating scrape that skimmed the dust to drifting clouds. Dori groaned at the sudden shaft of his scream that echoed eerily and died in a gasping groan behind the crash of the timber as the man released it.

'Lucky I happened by,' he said, wiping the sweat from his brow. 'Another hour and that rafter would've been his coffin.'

'Lucky?' gasped Dori. 'Mister, that weren't no luck, not in my book it weren't. That was — ' She shuddered as the man bent again to pick up the girl's dress and run it through his fingers. 'It was that, the dress . . . '

'Yeah,' drawled the man, 'I heard. Belongs to the fella's gal, don't it? Tom Huckerman's daughter. That him?'

'Sure it does,' frowned Dori, 'and,

136

yep, this is Tom Huckerman. Yuh see, we were . . . ' She paused, her gaze tightening on the man's face. 'Yuh know him? Yuh some friend of his or somethin?'

'Sort of,' grinned the man.

'So who are yuh, and how come — ?'

'Name's Coyne, ma'am. Marshal Coyne. Pleased to meet yuh. Darn near most of yuh as it happened, eh?'

Dori flinched under the man's probing stare and fingered the poncho self-consciously. 'Yeah, well . . . ' She stiffened. 'I was kinda busy — just as I'm goin' to be right now tryin' to get this fella here back to somethin' like the livin'. Yuh goin' to give a hand?'

'Sure, ma'am. You just name it. I'm all for keepin' Tom Huckerman alive and greetin' him proper.'

Dori was shivering again as she came to kneel at Tom's side. She was near exhausted, catching fitfully at tight, anxious breath, in one moment elated in her relief at Tom's release from the rafter, in the next conscious of her glances at the staring Marshal Coyne.

He may have ridden into the ghost town like the answer to her prayers, but she had sure as hell not reckoned on him staying to haunt.

14

There was just enough of the lean morning light for Sheriff Ed Woods to make out the stragglings of the track through the smothering mounds of dark boulders. Another hour, he thought, and the sun would be up full and shimmering top of the high peaks and he could get to the real heart of the worries nagging at his bones.

Not that they would need any prompting. Damn it, the agony of them, had been there every minute of the long night. And a half of them was perched right here, back of him; the mound of rags clinging to his shirt like there would be no tomorrow.

He grunted and swallowed again as he gave the mount a looser rein to pick its way over a sweep of shale. But, then, he reasoned, could he blame the girl? She had risked everything, down to her last breath, in coming to him back there at Brenard's, telling him what she knew and slipping him the Colt. Some risk, save perhaps that she had nothing to lose. A hell-hole for the prospect of another coming up on just about any roll of the dice was no gamble.

More to the very immediate point so far as he was concerned, was what to do with the girl now. Hell, was there a choice? She was going to be there, back to him, clinging and swaying, sometimes letting her head fall to his shoulders, sometimes jerking into life as the track turned and twisted, for just as long as it took.

Only trouble was . . . *only* trouble? Make no mistake, there was a whole heap of it lying in wait! That two-bit scumbag, Coyne, for one. Well, no doubting now where he was heading and why, and a featherbed to a sack of straw that had been Tom Huckerman spoiling with the fellow, Mohawk Stein, with Dori Maguire, as the girl had since told him, in tow.

How had they teamed up, he wondered? No matter, the girl had also reckoned on another no-odds prospect: that it would take Brenard just one swallow and two spits of his cheap sourmash to put a couple of his trusted sidekicks on their tails.

'Brenard ain't for losin' out on so much as the dirt he steps in,' the girl had murmured at his back once they had ridden fast and hard from the shack and were deep into the shadows of the Broken Necks. 'He figures for y'self and that fella who watered up at his place for trackin' the fancy Colts shootist — and he wants the spoils of the lot of yuh. All he can lift once you're dead. He'll figure for the sidekicks handlin' that, but not 'til they can make it a one-stab attack. They'll wait 'til you're all as good as sittin' in each others' pockets. That's why he let yuh get away. Figured yuh'd break outa that shack sooner or later.'

'And y'self?' Ed had grunted. 'How come — '

'I been plannin' on tryin' for a break since a fella won Dori Maguire in a card game. She was my friend, such as yuh could have in a place like Brenard's. Looked to me, always had. When the scumbag carted her off, I got to plannin' serious. T'ain't that difficult for a gal in my line to get her hands on a Colt, but a gun ain't no use unless yuh got some place to go with it. Yuh'd only pull the trigger once in Brenard's sight. So, then you turned up, mister, and I figured yuh for — '

'I can imagine!'

'Do my best for yuh wherever yuh goin'. Try anyhow. And I'm grateful yuh reached for me like yuh did. If yuh hadn't . . . ' The girl had tightened her grip. 'Folk call me Perdy, and I been holed up with Brenard for what seems like a lifetime.'

And it showed, thought Ed, bringing the mount to a walking pace over loose rocks. Still, she was here now and no going back, *and* she knew these mountain tracks and where they might be leading.

She had also brought the Colt, greased and full loaded. And that did matter some.

Now all he had to do was stay ahead of Brenard's trailing sidekicks and catch up with the bogus marshal before he got to Tom Huckerman.

Main street in Trulso would be quiet as a mouse in soft socks right now, he mused, and some folk would be happy to see the sun come up.

And then he cursed as only a worried lawman knew how.

★　★　★

Dori Maguire had been mouthing her own curses for what seemed like hours. Cursing the leftover luck that had dogged her all her life, tripped her and double-crossed at every turn, and even now, just when she had thought she might be free of one seething hell, pitched her headlong into another.

And it was beginning to rub off.

Damn it, Tom Huckerman might have been a whole lot more fortunate had he not been sheltering against the storm in that overhang and heard Stotts venting his drunken anger, and he might have made a darn sight faster progress if he had not insisted on looking to her and bringing her along of him. And maybe this, the trap he had been lured into at Morton, would have been avoided if she, the luckless Dori Maguire, had not been there to jinx him.

Or was she lathering herself into self-pity?

Could be she was, and could be she should bury her own woes and get back to the practical needs — like tending the fellow here and making sure he stayed breathing, and, not least, keeping a close eye on the reach of the shadow pacing through the first of the early light not a dozen yards away.

The shadow most of all.

She flinched into life as Tom stirred

at her knees and dabbed once again at the sweat standing like rain across his cheeks and brow. She was reckoning on the luck having held against him breaking any bones in the fall, but the cuts, bruising and now a high fever were taking their toll. Might be days, she figured, before he was in any fit state to get to his feet and stay there. Days too late as far as closing on the raiders was concerned.

Best Tom Huckerman might find himself left with come a week was a body set to split at the slightest movement, his daughter's crucifix and chain, her torn, stained dress and a two-bit tart in a sackcloth poncho.

She flinched again as the shadow came to rest in the splintered gap in the one-time store's frontage. Now what, she wondered? If that Marshal Coyne got to asking her once more how the fellow was doing, she would spit clean in his face! Hell, he could see for himself well enough, so why the hurry, why the impatience? Anybody would think he *needed* Tom back on his feet.

Well, she thought, maybe he did at that.

He had offered no more in explanation of how he had come to be in the Broken Necks and by chance trailing into a ghost town when he did save to say that he was a long-time friend of Tom Huckerman's, had heard of the homestead raid while passing through Trulso and decided to lend an old friend a hand.

'Figured he'd head north,' he had said. 'Safest place for scumbags holdin' a young gal. Seems I was right.'

No arguing against that, Dori had reasoned, sort of thing that was understood between friends, and a full-blown lawman standing to Tom was not to be sneezed at should he ever get to the raiders. That was a real piece of luck. Even so . . .

Damn it, there was no excusing the way he looked at her, specially not in a situation bleak as this, no fathoming either the gleam in his eyes when he stared at Tom. That was no behaviour fitting to a marshal and a whole sight too eager between friends. In fact, thinking it through, there was a deal about Marshal Coyne that bothered her.

Dori's fingers spread almost without her being conscious of the movement to the girl's dress. Just what, she wondered, had been Tom's thoughts in the moment of reaching for it? He must have —

She gulped on a sudden intake of breath as Tom's left eye sprung open as if shutters had been torn from a lantern-lit window.

'Not a sound,' he hissed through dry, cracked lips. 'And don't move. Just don't turn yuh back on that fella there, and keep them guns of mine close. Yuh hear?'

Dori swallowed and nodded.

'Coyne's here to kill us. First chance he gets.'

And then the eye closed again and

Tom Huckerman lay still and silent as the grave.

* ★ * ★ * ★ *

Four hours now of blazing sun, thick shadows and a mountain range that loomed like a basking monster, and still no signs of another life, not up ahead of him, not to the back of him; nothing save the drift of a lone hawk, the rattle and slither of a hunting snake, the girl's hot breath on his neck, clip of hoofs, jangle of tack and the grunts that came with his thoughts.

Sheriff Woods narrowed his already squinting gaze on the track. How many more miles, how many hours before he got to picking up so much as the scantiest hint of Coyne, he wondered? How many days, damn it, before he got to Tom Huckerman, if he ever did and if, even then, there would be anything left of the fellow worth the picking over? Reputed top gunman Tom might have been in his day, but that was years back, and ten of them spent home-steading in the dirt of the Trulso plain was no fitting warm up for a return — with or without 'fancy Colts'. And just where had he had them stashed all these years?

Sometimes, you never knew the half of a fellow.

And when it came to reckoning miles and hours, how many were Brenard's men away? They would have moved fast, anxious to get their quarry in view soon as it was light. But then what? Trail it out in the shadows? Watch and wait? No point in striking too early; no good to be had either in leaving it too late. So maybe . . .

'Place called Morton up ahead,' murmured Perdy over Ed's shoulder. 'Ghost town. But I been there one time. Dragged through it more like on my way to Brenard's. T'ain't much, but the sorta hole a runnin' man might head for. Got water along of it.'

'Brenard's men know of it?' asked Ed.

'They'd know, sure enough. Not a deal they don't know to hereabouts. Rats know their own trash, don't they? We makin' for Morton?'

'Do we have a choice?' grunted Ed, easing the tired mount to a gentle slope. 'Horse here ain't for much further.'

'Same went for somebody else,' quipped the girl loosening a hand to point to the curl of soft smoke in the far distance. 'That's Morton.'

15

'He goin' to make it, or yuh want for me to start diggin'?' The man stepped carefully through the shafted sunlight, halted in the shadows of the debris and gazed like a perching hawk at the body sprawled across the dust. 'Don't look too good,' he mouthed, pushing aside the tails of his dust-coat with an impatient flick.

'He'll be fine, just fine,' said Dori Maguire hurriedly. 'Just don't pester. He needs time.' Her hands fidgeted over Tom Huckerman's shirt as she shifted her kneeling position. 'Another hour or so.'

'Another hour or so and that kid of his could be dead as this place,' drawled Coyne, flicking at the coat again.

'Yuh that concerned about the girl why don't yuh go do somethin' about it?' snapped Dori. 'Damn it, you're his friend, aren't yuh?'

Coyne's gaze narrowed darkly. 'Gettin' a mite short-lipped there, lady,' he said. 'Mebbe I should remind yuh if it hadn't been for me — '

'Yeah, yeah, I know. Hadn't been for you he'd be like as not cold dead. I ain't unaware of that and I guess he won't be neither when he comes to — *when* he comes to.' Dori adjusted the drape of the poncho. 'So why don't yuh quit the starin' and go get some fresh coffee brewin' on that fire yuh lit out there? Yuh can leave Mr Huckerman to me.'

'That a fact?' grinned Coyne. 'My, yuh have a way of bein' real bossy when yuh've a mind, ma'am, and that's for sure. Now, personally speakin', I like a woman with a touch of spirit. Kinda gives her an edge, don't it? But, then, comin' from where yuh have — '

'What yuh sayin', mister?' flared Dori, her eyes gleaming. 'What yuh mean '*where I've come from*'? What's it to yuh? I ain't said nothin' about comin' from nowhere. Not a word. So what yuh inferrin'? Yuh ain't never set eyes on me before — and likewise — so there ain't no chance of yuh knowin' . . . ' She paused, her gaze burning. 'Not unless — '

'Brenard's,' grinned Coyne. 'One of his stable, weren't yuh? Oh, sure, I heard. Called by the dump on my way here. Fella you and Huckerman never got to finishin' was shootin' his mouth. So, like I say — '

'Yuh ain't no marshal,' sneered Dori. 'Nothin' like. Just who the hell are yuh, mister?'

Coyne eased a slow hand down the dust-coat. 'Gal like you don't need no name, does she? Fella's a fella, take 'em and leave 'em. Yuh had one, yuh had 'em all, eh?'

'Sonofabitch!'

'Now you goin' on some about time and havin' plenty of it before good old Tom Huckerman there comes to, gets me to thinkin' we should . . . ' Coyne's grin slid away as he turned sharply to the glare of sunlight beyond the debris.

'What's that? Yuh hear?'

'I heard,' said Dori, coming slowly to her feet. 'Horses. Movin' horses. And they ain't ours, are they?'

'Fetched yours and Huckerman's in an hour back. Watered up and hitched along of mine out there in the street,' croaked Coyne, moving stealthily through the shadows to the brightness.

'Then I'd say we got company, wouldn't you?' said Dori as lightly as the cold cling of the shiver through her body would let her. 'Mebbe them raider fellas back again checkin' on their handiwork. Mebbe yuh should go take a look, *Mister Marshal*!'

* * *

'Don't do nothin' stupid. Just play along with him.'

Dori stifled another gulp and shiver at the hissed, half-strangled words from the body sprawled in the shadow of the fallen rafter. 'Yuh hearin' me?' hissed Tom again, one eye flicking open.

'I hear yuh,' whispered Dori. Her fingers twisted nervously over the poncho. 'But supposin' — '

'Supposin' nothin'! Do as I say!'

Dori swallowed, wiped a wet, sticky hand down a damp, sweating cheek and stepped like a nervous cat through the mess of timbers to where Coyne hovered on the edge of the sun blaze.

'See anythin'?' she asked, risking a furtive glance back to the body.

'Only one horse,' murmured Coyne, squinting into the glare. 'Gettin' closer. Can't make out . . . ' His hand brushed aside the dust-coat and fell to the butt of his holstered Colt. The squinting gaze tightened. A shoulder muscle flexed.

Dori risked another glance backward. Tom was still motionless, eyes closed, not so much as a twitch through his body, but his right hand had moved, sure enough, a couple of inches closer to his gunbelt. Just how in the name of reason did he figure he could for one moment . . . ?

'Stand clear,' snapped Coyne, drawing his Colt as he strode the few steps from the wreck of the store to the street.

Sun was at his back; he had an edge there, thought Dori. Whoever it was riding in would see Coyne as no more than a blurred, shimmering shape as he struggled through watering eyes for the sight of a face. Might be a whole stack of vital minutes before he got to seeing Coyne clear. Maybe minutes too late if the so-called marshal got to using that Colt.

And he would, you bet he would, if he was here to kill Tom Huckerman in his time, his way. Hardly be relishing an audience, damn it!

Dori's swallow stuck like a rock in her throat. Sweat oozed across her shoulders, trickled hot and then icy down her back. Her head refused to turn for another glance. What, in God's name, was back of Tom Huckerman's mind?

Hell, she thought, clearing the

swallow as if drinking cold lead, she was wallowing way out of her depth.

'Hold it, mister, right there,' called Coyne, gesturing with the Colt. 'Yuh come far enough. Too damned far! Figured I'd left yuh for stewin' back there in Trulso. So how come yuh got this curious?'

'Know something, *Marshal* Coyne,' drawled Ed Woods, reining the mount to a snorting halt, 'we long-toothed sheriffs get to sleepin' light at nights. We get to thinkin', and I sure as a dog's breakfast got to thinkin' a heap about you.'

'Nasty habit,' grinned Coyne.

'Too late for breakin' it now.' Ed drew tight on the reins. 'I figured yuh, mister. Scaffs Coyne, right? Got to drinkin' both sides of the glass. Law-swinger. Did time in the Pen. Frank's brother, sure enough, but yuh ain't rootin' in Tom Huckerman's shadow just to ask him how your kin died. Oh, no, far from it. Yuh plan on killin' him. I got it right, *Mister* Coyne?'

Dori cringed and shuffled closer to the sunlight, her head buzzing with unanswered questions: the sheriff out of Trulso, here, but how come, and just how . . . ? She gulped on another rock-hard swallow as she peered into the street to see a worn, dust-locked fellow easing from his horse then turning to lend a hand to the woman mounted up back of him. Perdy! Damn it, how had she . . . ?

'Right, fella. Right as yuh'll ever get,' sneered Coyne, levelling the Colt. 'But yuh should've stayed nursin' the shadows 'stead of meddlin'. T'ain't done yuh one mite of good, has it, 'cus there ain't no way you're goin' to ride outa this hole alive? But I guess yuh already figured that.'

'I figured a whole lot, mister, best of all being — '

Ed Woods swayed, steadied himself against the mount, pushed at the brim of his hat and dripped sweat freely to the dirt. 'What the hell!' he groaned.

Dori blinked and swung round at the

sound of a scuffed step far end of the debris.

Coyne's steady gaze snapped from the sheriff to the same sound.

'Well, now,' croaked Tom Huckerman, his back tight to a standing post of the one-time store veranda, Colts drawn and steady in both hands, face as pinched and grey as wagon canvas, eyes crow-sharp in their stare, 'ain't we just got some party here?'

★   ★   ★

Ed Woods had taken a half-step from his mount, Perdy reaching for him; Coyne had swung his Colt on his new target and eased the trigger pressure; Dori stumbled in the debris and clawed blindly for support, and Tom Huckerman barely moved when the blaze and then the echoing whine of rifle shots split the sunlit silence like the roar of sudden flame.

Ed froze, grabbed Perdy and dived for the nearest cover. Coyne lifted the dust in his rush for the shadows. Dori fell back in the debris, her poncho sodden with sweat. Tom squinted into the tumbled peaks of the mounts and dropped instinctively to one knee.

'Brenard's men,' yelled Ed, from his cover behind a mound of splintered crates. 'Two of 'em. Been trailin' us.'

Coyne cursed and slid into deeper shade.

Dori lay still.

Tom shuffled on his heels to the bones of a smashed wagon. 'Hold yuh fire,' he called. 'Let 'em move in.'

The clouding dust settled. Silence fell heavy and stifling. The street shimmered in the high sun haze and Dori Maguire blinked through cold sweat where she crouched in the shadows of the debris.

A town sheriff, a bogus, gunslinging marshal, a bewildered bar girl, a near broken man obsessed with the hunt for his kidnapped daughter . . . and now, as if the mix needed a spark, two of

Brenard's sidekicks sharpening up for a shoot-out.

Hell, she thought, with Tom Huckerman around who needed action!

She swallowed, eased the sticky poncho clear of her bare skin beneath it, and crept forward slowly, her gaze moving over the rocky slopes and overhangs surrounding the ghost town. Brenard's men might be anywhere, behind any one of a hundred mounds, skulking like dogs through the shadows of clefts and narrow creeks, waiting and watching from the cover of boulders.

All very well for Huckerman to sit it out till the scum-bags moved in, she mused, but would they? Damn it, what was to stop them laying siege to the tumbledown timbers that had once been Morton for as long as it suited; maybe call up more guns; do nothing till the time when their quarry had to do something?

And meantime, would Coyne see his chance and turn his Colt on Tom Huckerman? If killing the fellow was his sole reason for trailing these dry bones mountains, Fate had dealt him the best hand he might ever see. All he had to do was slip from those shadows to the back of that broken wagon where Tom was crouched, and before you could blink . . .

Dori blinked, sure enough, a dozen sweat-swimming times as she watched the man who had ridden in with Perdy back of him step into the street and stand his ground like a man with a death-wish.

16

'Of all the darn fool things to do! Damnit, Ed, this ain't Trulso!' Tom Huckerman spat the words and eased his limbs against the throb of bruising pain. 'Get the hell back,' he hissed, squinting against the glare as Ed Woods settled his stance in the deserted street, arms loose, body straight and stiff. Fellow had to be out of his mind to reckon on drawing the sidekicks out of the rocks. He was offering a clean target, easy as holing a barrel at two paces.

Tom winced at the crack of the first shot, then opened his eyes wide and staring as Ed crashed like a felled, lone-standing pine to the dirt.

'Hell!' he hissed, again, swallowing on a gravel throat. Only consolation to come out of that madness was to pinpoint exactly where the sidekick had fired from; and if Ed Woods had reckoned his life worth no more than —

Tom cleared his throat and grinned softly. 'Wily old coot!' he murmured. Fellow was no more dead than the flies already buzzing round him! He had reckoned the distance, figured the risk and judged that a single shot to a sun-blurred shape would odds on pass him; at worst, wing him. He had stayed lucky, but how long could he feign a dead body out there? How long before the flies pestered him crazy? How long before the sidekick decided to make certain he had not missed?

That was going to be a risk too far.

Tom swung his gaze to the collapsed store. Dori Maguire had collected Stotts's Winchester. Did she still have it, was it close? With fire power like that in his hands he might just level the edge. Sure, but could he get to her? He might if Coyne were not covering him. Some chance! All that sonofabitch was doing was waiting on Huckerman making a move — and planning on it being his last.

'Goddamnit!' he cursed, easing his limbs again and thinking for one uneasy moment that Ed had twitched.

*   *   *

Dori scrambled back through the maze of timbers to where Tom had lain. The Winchester, she had hidden it a reach away against Coyne's unhealthy ideas getting the better of him. No one had seen it, maybe not even Tom, but he sure as hell needed it now with that fool fellow lying stiff as a plank and Brenard's men doubtless moving closer.

'Get it,' she mouthed. 'Just get it and get out there!'

Dori had retrieved the rifle and was crawling to the sunlight again when a boot thudded across the barrel and a line of hot spittle sizzled through the dust.

'Busy lady, ain't yuh?' sneered Coyne, hovering over her like a mantling grey hawk. 'So where yuh goin' with that? Not to our good friend, Mr Huckerman, surely? Oh, no, lady, that yuh ain't.' He scraped his boot along the gleaming steel. 'No, yuh stayin' right here where I can keep an eye on yuh. Mr Huckerman wants that rifle there he'll have to come and get it, won't he?'

★   ★   ★

The shadows, damn it, the shadows — find them, hug them, use them same as you did a hundred times way back. Had them on your side then, so put them to work again. You know how; all you got to do is remember.

Tom slid slowly, carefully, tentative as a beetle on hot stones, from the shade of the wagon towards the collapsed store. No sight or sound of Dori, but she was there, sure enough, that Winchester along of her. Now all he had to hope was that Brenard's men dallied in the boulders long enough for him to reach her, that Ed Woods stayed stiff and that Coyne had not got two steps ahead of him. No sight or sound of him either. Not surprising. Scaffs Coyne was no stranger to shadows.

Tom swallowed, gritted his teeth and eased on. No shortage of shadows; any amount among the bones of the ghost town, each one cooler, deeper than the last as he approached the one-time store, working his way steadily towards the rear of it, trusting that he would find a gap just big enough to squeeze through.

He paused to glance back at the street. Ed was still there, sprawled in the dirt, not so much as a finger moving, but surrounded now by an inquisitive swirl of flies. How much longer before they got too intense for him? And just where was the girl who had ridden back of him? Curled in a ball in the deepest cover she could find if she had any sense.

Tom swallowed again, winced at the throbbing pain and dragged himself another few yards, close enough now to the store to peer into its silent gloom. Too damned silent, he thought, the sort of silence you got to listening to; the sort that seemed to be filled with something waiting.

Somebody.

Another yard. Time running out now. Brenard's men would be set to move; Ed would be going quietly mad; Coyne getting impatient.

He pressed himself tight to the store's broken timbers. Space here wide enough to slide through, he reckoned. Just ease into it, through the mesh of cobwebs, the haze of dust, take it slowly over the creaks, watch for anything rotten that might collapse; one steady step, pause, listen, watch, another step . . .

'Not bad for a fella your age and state,' drawled Coyne from somewhere in the gloom ahead. 'But yuh go real gentle now, Tom Huckerman. Real gentle. I gotta body here I ain't for spoilin' unless yuh get careless, and spoil I surely will if I don't see them Colts easin' to the floor like dead moths. Yuh got it?'

Tom licked at the sweat trickling to his mouth. 'What yuh want, Coyne?' he croaked. 'Not that I need ask. Yuh ain't still sweatin' over that sonofabitch brother of yours I had the pleasure of takin' out, are yuh? Yuh pickin' over bad bones there, Scaffs.'

'Shut yuh lips, Huckerman! Yuh ain't in no position for mouthin'. I got the deck and I'm dealin'.'

'Reckon so, but what yuh ain't figured — '

Tom fell back at the splintering crack and whine of rifles blazing into life beyond the store. Brenard's men moving in. No chance now for Ed. No chance for anybody unless . . .

He drew his Colts in one swift reach, regardless now of Coyne, where he was or what he might be planning next, and let their roar rip through the mass of shattered timbers like streaks of flame. There was a scream from the deepest of the shadows, a grunted curse, and then the crash of footfalls and a scrambling body.

More rifle shots. Another scream. Timbers being thrown aside.

Coyne was making a break for it!

Tom crashed forward, only to stumble over Dori Maguire as she squirmed for tighter cover.

'To yuh right!' she gasped, collapsing against the rafter. 'He's headin' back to the street.'

The hell he was, but too fast for Tom to drag his throbbing limbs in pursuit. Nothing else for it, let the rat run and concentrate on Brenard's men.

Tom staggered to his left and the gap to the sunlit street. He blinked furiously against the drifts of dust and gunshot smoke, then narrowed his gaze for shapes, the faintest blur of something moving, anything that might be the figure of a man.

But who? A Brenard sidekick, or a risen Ed Woods?

'Hell!' he groaned, and scuffed a few steps on to the edge of the glare.

'Over here!'

Ed's yell echoed from the shell of a building across the street.

'Got yuh,' shouted Tom. 'Watch out for Coyne. He's pullin' out!'

The sweat broke across his back like a tide. He swallowed deep and hard on a throat as cracked as scorched leather, blinked again and weighed the Colts heavy as rocks in his sticky hands. Ed's mock death had worked God alone knew how — but where was Coyne and, more to the point in the new sullen silence that had slipped over the place like a cloak, where were Brenard's men?

He turned slowly from the glare, conscious of Dori Maguire's eyes gleaming her fear through the gloom. He could almost hear her shivers, feel the chill across her bones, but she nodded a response to his gesture for silence.

Tom swallowed again, eased the

Colts a fraction higher and concentrated on the jumbled mass of shadows. Had Brenard's men stayed together or split — one watching the street while the other scouted the broken-down buildings? Would Ed stay holed up or get to stalking Coyne? Scaffs had never been for risking a crowded field. He would be clear of Morton first chance he had, scattering like dust to the mountains, content to wait on his reckoning till another time, another place.

What the hell, he thought, Scaffs Coyne could scatter all he liked and wait till he rotted, there was a business to be settled here and now, and fast, and a trail out there waiting on him.

There was Holly.

She had been here, right here, maybe on this very spot, in that dress, the one he had bought in Trulso on that summer's afternoon.

The sweat trickled suddenly cold and flat cross his cheeks. He glanced at Dori's gleaming eyes, her hands gripping the Winchester, whitening the knuckles, listened, and eased a slow step forward.

He winced at the creak of a timber, took another step and held it half settled, half suspended at the movement of a shadow ahead of him. His eyes narrowed. The shadow grew, spreading like a long black stain, twisting and folding over the debris, then pausing, waiting.

'Come on, come on,' he mouthed, lifting the Colt in his right hand, blinking on the sweat at his eyes.

The silence broke like something crushed underfoot as the shadow swung towards him, seemed for a moment to sprawl there and then thickened in the shape of the man behind it.

'We ain't takin' no prisoners,' growled the voice.

'Same here — no space for 'em!' snapped Tom, seconds before he released the full, searing blaze of the Colts and watched, his eyes wide and round now, as the man was flung back over the debris and cluttered timbers, dust and clinging cobwebs shrouding his fall.

'Behind yuh!' screamed Dori from the gloom.

Tom swung round, the guns still tight in his hands.

The Colts were roaring again almost before the fellow catching the blast of them had stepped from the glare of the street to the shadowed store, certainly long before he had so much as a glimpse of the hands gripping them, and he was already staring lifelessly when he hit the dirt a yard ahead of a fly-bitten, sweat-soaked Ed Woods.

'Can see yuh been takin' some shootin' lessons, Tom Huckerman,' croaked the sheriff. 'Learn fast, don't yuh!'

17

'Said it before, say it again: you're plain mule-headed stubborn, and that's the fact of it! Ain't no other way of seein' it, not from where I'm standin' there ain't.' Ed Woods kicked at the dirt and brought the boot down with a heavy thud. He sighed, grunted, swept the sweat from his brow and fixed the man saddling up the mount with a tight but not unsympathetic stare. 'For God's sake, Tom,' he began again, 'time's come — '

Tom Huckerman gave the girth a final tug and patted the mare affectionately. 'Yuh right, Ed, time has come, and right now I'm wastin' it.'

'Yuh'll be countin' it down to yuh grave if yuh don't listen up there!' croaked Ed, settling his hands on his hips. 'Goddamn it, Tom, yuh just ain't in no state to go on. Look at yuh, hardly a bone in yuh body that ain't grindin' like some three-wheeled wagon. And look at them cuts and bruisin', not to mention ... hell, a fella don't have half a buildin' fall on him and step clear like he was slippin' from a featherbed!'

He turned to gaze over the deepening shadows spreading through the mountain peaks, and rubbed a hand across his stubbled chin. 'We come outa this better than we should have when yuh get to reckonin'. Had ourselves some fair luck there, but that ain't to say — '

'Yuh ran that 'playing dead' trick a mite close,' snapped Tom.

'It worked, didn't it?' said Ed, turning sharply. 'Brought them scumbags outa the rocks. Made 'em think they were three parts home and dry.'

'Coyne could've got to yuh.'

'But he didn't, did he? Only thought uppermost in his mind was kickin' the dust 'tween us and him. Rat! But he'll be waitin' on yuh, sure enough. Oh, yes, he's out there, and minute he claps an eye on yuh it'll be lead spittin' faster than a whipped whore. Yuh know that well as I do. Yuh know why he's here, don't yuh? He spelled that out big as a barn door.'

'I know,' murmured Tom. 'I've always known.'

'Sure yuh have. And now *I* know.'

Tom leaned on the mount for a moment, then eased round to face Ed as if turning to a voice recognized from long back. 'I was all through with them days, Ed. Gave 'em up minute I met May. But I ain't f'gotten nothin', not a thing, and if that's goin' to be the way to get to Holly, so be it.' His stare darkened. 'I ain't for doubtin' that for a second, and that's somethin' yuh know well as I do. I kill easy when there's good need, Ed, and that's another fact, plain as yuh'll get. Sorry. Didn't intend no deception and wouldn't have strapped these Colts on again if . . . Yeah, well, that don't need no spellin' out neither.'

'Listen up there, I ain't for carin' or

botherin' about yuh past one spit. What yuh were, what yuh done, is past, and I'm leavin' it right there. But I ain't lettin' you ride into them rocks in that state when there's a crazed dog intent on revenge watchin' for yuh and a handful of lice as anxious to see yuh dead. Ain't nothin' for Holly, Tom, if she gets to hear you're crow meat.

'So,' grunted Ed, stamping his boot again, 'I'm comin' with yuh — and no arguing! Let yuh ride outa Trulso when I shouldn't have, and I sure as hell ain't come this far to ride back. Nossir. We settle these womenfolk we seem to have acquired best we can 'til we get back — *if* we get back — then we go reckon with Coyne and them raiders. T'ain't one man's job, not even when he's the likes of Tom Huckerman. This may be your show, but we're doin' it t'gether. And there's another fact.'

'And here's another, mister!'

The men turned to the heavier evening shadows creeping like old ghosts from the ruined buildings as Dori Maguire and Perdy sauntered from them to the spread of last light.

'Overlookin' somethin', ain't yuh?' asked Dori, cradling the Winchester in her arms. 'Well, ain't yuh?'

'I just said — ' groaned Ed.

'Yeah, yeah, we heard what yuh said, Mr Woods. Couldn't do no other way yuh were mouthin' there. But it don't suit.' She hunched the rifle into the folds of the poncho. 'We — me and Perdy here — ain't for stayin'. Not nowhere. We're comin' with yuh.'

'Now hold on there — ' spluttered Ed.

'Tell 'em, Perdy,' snapped Dori.

'Like she says, we ain't for stayin'. Could be Brenard might get to lookin' for his sidekicks, and that ain't no prospect we fancy. So we reckon as how yuh could mebbe use — '

'Gal, yuh just ain't got no idea, not a notion, of what we could be ridin' into up there in them hills,' flared Ed. 'I'm tellin' yuh, fellas we're dealin' with are mangy as hounds in a flea-pit.'

'We been dealin' with the likes of 'em better part of a lifetime, mister,' drawled Dori, slipping her weight to one hip. 'And in ways that'd make yuh hair stand stiff. So what we don't know about fellas, 'specially scumbags, ain't worth a tin can. No, we figure yuh could use us, mebbe get to needin' us. And, 'sides, I owe Mr Huckerman, and Perdy stands to yuh debt, Sheriff, for bringin' her outa Brenard's. Might say we're payin' yuh back, pair of yuh. Yuh get it?'

'No, I don't!' grunted Ed.

'Well, try!' clipped Dori. 'Meantime, we rounded up the mounts, sorted whatever's worth the takin' and figure we're all set to ride. Should make good miles cover of dark. What yuh say, Mr Huckerman?'

'I wouldn't be arguin', ma'am,' murmured Tom, turning back to the mount. 'Time's come for ridin'.'

'But, hell — ' began Ed.

'But nothin', mister,' smiled Dori. 'If

180

Mr Huckerman is for ridin', we're ridin'. Don't pay to cross him, does it?'

★　★　★

The party that finally cleared the brooding, gloom-shadowed silence of the ghost town a half-hour later might have looked, from the grim set of faces, the fixed, steady gazes, that they meant business wherever they might find it. But the truth of it, for at least three of them, was a whole lot different.

Ed Woods had fumed and fretted, sweated and argued till his throat was parched, the sweat running cold and his mind in a whirl.

There had been no reasoning with this Tom Huckerman, that much he had learned fast, just as he had back there in Trulso. And when he came to it, where was the man who could, or would? No, Tom had his destiny staring him in the face — and the fellow was not for blinking and just about as far from being the hard-working home-steader on a soul-breaking plain as he could get.

Tom Huckerman had slipped back a dozen years and into the life of the twin Colts gunslinger with all the ease and instinct of pulling on a well-worn gun glove. Only problem twitching through Ed's mind was would the homesteader find it just as easy to throw the glove aside when the business was done? If he could. Damn it, if he wanted to! Never any telling where a fellow might tread when he stepped back. Never no knowing where he might head.

Had the bogus Marshal Coyne figured that, he wondered, or was the sonofabitch too blinkered to see further than the Boot Hill marker to his brother's grave and standing in the shadow of it?

Might not be more than a few night hours to him finding out.

And then — oh, yes, and then, Ed had muttered more than once — there were the women.

Dori Maguire was not for tangling with and probably had more than a fair notion of how to use that Winchester she cradled like a babe. She was for standing to her own ground now that she had found it along of Tom. Look to her peppering your butt with hot shot if you stepped into it!

But Perdy — just who, when the going got rough, was going to look to her? Sure, she had covered herself well enough against Brenard's sidekicks, thanks to the debris and tumbledowns of the old town, but next time there might not be such handy cover and nowhere to run to.

Best face it, he had reckoned with another sigh, the girl was his responsibility. And he needed that like he needed a sore head — which he had anyhow!

Ed had gone back then to watching the line of riders and the gathering night in its sweep from the mountain peaks. Not a deal of comfort in either, he had thought.

Dori was grateful for once for the spreading mass of the makeshift poncho. It hid her shivering. And she *was* shivering. No, not against the chill night air; not because of what had happened back there at Morton; not even at the thought of the staring Marshal Coyne and what he might have done given the spit of a half chance.

She was shivering in her recall of the look in Tom Huckerman's eyes at the sight of Holly's dress hanging from the rafter. The look that in a moment had been so filled with hope, almost relief, only to darken as if at the onset of a violent storm. A look then that had darkened, thickened, built like a rock face of cloud and been set alight by hatred.

Tom Huckerman had been hating since the day of the raid at the homestead and the realization of his loss — she had seen that clear enough in his look minute he had begun his story — but now it was deeper, tighter and festering in him like a bad growth.

It had been there in the shooting of Brenard's men, there in his stare into the eyes of Scaffs Coyne; there, too, when he folded the dress and slid it into his saddle-bag, when he had reached to his pocket for the crucifix and fixed it to his own neck, and was there right now, she could sense, in the eyes watching for the trail as the night closed in. And it would be there, you could bet, come sun-up.

There was a deal to be said for a spreading poncho, she thought, stifling another shiver.

18

Five, ten, twenty miles — hell, a fellow could keep going forever and still not see a half of the Broken Necks, let alone know them, thought Ed, easing his aching butt against the slip and slide of the mount beneath him. And why this obsession with holding to a trail north? Anybody would have thought for Tom Huckerman knowing exactly where he was heading, when the truth of it was he probably had no better notion of where the homestead raiders were planning on fetching up than the track could tell him.

Precious little, mused Ed, not unless he had some powers not given to most men for reading a shift of dust through a drift of pebbles.

Fact was, the scumbags could head in almost any direction to almost any place they chose — just so long as they

186

finally had a buyer for the girl, always assuming she was still in any fit state to fetch a price.

Coyne, on the other hand, would be heading nowhere special. His only concern would be to keep Tom in his sights until the time came to make his move.

But not in this light, grunted Ed to his thoughts, with only the softest glimmer of breaking cloud far to the east. No, Coyne would wait. He had the edge. He was dealing. And that could sure as hell get messy if he got to picking them off from some high cover. Might make a deal more sense . . .

Tom was reining up, bringing his mount round in a slow circle to face the line. And not before time! Ed ran a hand over his dirt-sticky neck and moved closer.

'I been figurin',' he began. 'We'd be a whole lot better placed if we — '

'Yuh take charge here, Ed,' said Tom. 'Keep to the same track. I'm splittin'. Goin' up ahead.'

'Oh, no, yuh ain't!' snapped Ed. 'Not without me along of yuh. Nossir. Don't make no sense to go it alone.'

'No arguin'. I ain't for havin' Scaffs Coyne waitin' on the light for a first shot. Time we got rid of him.'

'Oh, sure,' mocked Ed, pulling at the reins. 'Just like that, eh? Just walk up to the fella and put a bullet 'tween his eyes. I'm all for that, Tom Huckerman, but I got this naggin' doubt that the double-dealing marshal ain't goin' to be quite so fussed.'

'He did it before,' murmured Dori. 'Back there. One of them scum was sittin' on our tails. Not any more. I seen it.'

'I don't give a damn what yuh saw. I'm sayin' as how — '

'Wastin' time, Ed,' said Tom, bringing his mount round again. 'I ain't for that. Yuh know what to do. Don't have to spell it out, do I?'

'But damnit, Tom, yuh just can't go — '

'Give me an hour, then yuh come

lookin'. Meantime, yuh stay on the track. No strayin', not for nothin'.'

Ed sank back in the saddle as Tom moved away to the shadows. 'Of all the mule-headed . . . ' he sighed, but fell silent under Dori Maguire's soft wink and slow smile.

'Come on, Perdy,' she said, taking a new grip on the pack mount back of her, 'let's get to what we do best — doin' as the man says!'

Ed Woods could only sigh again and tug impatiently at the reins.

★ ★ ★

The half light was near perfect; only the silence that hung in waiting as if to be summoned worried Tom as he brought the mount to a slow, measured walk once clear of Ed and the women. Even so, he rode on for another twenty minutes before reining up in the deepest cover of a lift of sharp crags, hitching the mare and slipping softly from the saddle to the cool, stony ground.

Just how far had Coyne strayed from the ghost town, he wondered? Smart fellow intent on a killing out here in the mountain wilderness would stay within sniffing distance of the narrow trail; out of sight but close enough to keep a watchful eye through the night on his quarry. But a smart fellow would sure as sun-up have spotted that one had gone missing since the first crack of light.

So where would the smart fellow be right now? And just how smart was his thinking?

Scaffs Coyne had been smart in his day, shrewd enough to double deal both sides of the law till his greed got too big for his appetite. But being that smart had been honed on lining his saddle-bags. Now, out here in the morning chill of the Broken Necks, he had only revenge on the table.

Fellow might just get to being loose fingered in that sort of a deal. Family matters could raise a man's blood to the boil when it should be running cold with a killing at stake.

Tom smoothed a steady hand over the mount's neck and turned away to climb the few feet into the crags that would give him a view of the emerging sweep of rocks.

He was sweating in spite of the dawn chill, and wincing through clenched teeth against the stabs and throb of the bruising across his body as he settled, flat on a craggy overhang, and moved his gaze through a slow, sweeping arc.

Darn near hardly a breath out there let alone a movement, he thought, blinking against the sting of the chill, the blades of breaking light that cut across the lift and fall of the land. Fellow might bury himself in the drifts and bulges of shadow and stay hidden for hours. And Coyne would know that. He would be figuring maybe right now that all he had to do was watch and wait; no call to move, not till he was good and ready, every step planned and plotted, certain of striking fast and foolproof.

Trouble being, Huckerman would not be there.

Tom swallowed. Had Scaffs already spotted the gap in the trailing party? Would that prompt an early move? A careless move? Could be he was already moving, skulking through the rocks like some dark, hungry animal. Any one of the shadows down there might be the one that would move, creep into a fellow's path without him ever knowing, not till it was a whole blaze of lead too late.

So why give him the edge?

Time to move, get this miserable episode off his back, get to . . . He ran his fingers over the crucifix at his neck. Somewhere in the chilled, dead silence of another day Holly was opening her eyes and wondering . . . Or shivering in her fear.

Tom's hands had flattened again on the rock, his gaze begun to blur on his thoughts when he tensed, blinked, gripped the jagged rim of the lift and pulled himself higher.

There was a shadow out there that had no reason to be where it was, that had not been there a minute ago and looked all set to move again.

'Oh, yes, mister, I got yuh,' he murmured, peering harder and deeper. 'I sure as hell got yuh! So you just keep right on movin'.'

He tensed again as the shadow slid on, passing quickly to Tom's left, pausing, waiting, shortening, squatter now, then lengthening, heading almost recklessly for a bulge of boulders above a sheer drop to the mountain track.

Tom's eyes narrowed as a frown creased his brow. If that was Coyne out there he was moving with a purpose in mind, some plan he had figured.

The boulders, damn it! Of course — Coyne was reckoning on setting up a spill of tumbling rocks to the trail, scattering and maybe killing Ed and the women, then turning his attention to the real quarry. And at this rate, he was going to be right alongside that bulge in a matter of minutes, before Tom had so much as slid clear of his cover.

'Sonofabitch!' he cursed in a gasp of breath, as he dropped to the ground with a thud that shot through his body like a sudden tremor.

He waited, gathering his strength, breathing long and deep, one hand smoothing the mount's neck, grunted and slid away to the nearest shadow. Light was breaking fast now, seeping over the night sky like trickles of fresh, cold milk. Soon there would be no place to hide save in the clutches of rock, no shadows to slip through — no way of reaching Coyne without him seeing the movement the second he was aware of it.

He kept moving, avoiding loose rocks, striding for the firmest and safest, wincing against the gnaw of his aches and bruises, pausing to listen for the creaks and grating of boulders being shifted.

All quiet so far. Maybe Ed was

holding to a slow pace and still too distant for Coyne to make his move. Maybe the boulders were too settled for moving. Maybe they never would. Sure, thought Tom, and maybe that breaking light up there would back off for an hour or so! Some chance. Could be the only decent thing to do was fire a warning shot, bring Ed and the women to a halt, divert Coyne's concentration. And offer himself as a target for good measure!

Tom paused again, cleared a wash of cold sweat, listened, one hand drifting like the light to the butt of a Colt. He narrowed his gaze over the broadening sky. Five minutes and the morning would sweep in like a thirsty herd to water. No holding it, no reckoning then on the cover of shadows.

He broke from a sprawl of rocks to an open spread that climbed to the bulge of boulders, scrambled to a halt and stiffened at the sight of Coyne, his body bent to the mass in a slithering, straining heave.

'Save yuh strength, Scaffs,' he called, his arms easy at his sides, hands loose above the Colts. 'T'ain't worth it. Not now it ain't.'

Coyne rested for a moment, his body still tensed against the mass, legs spread over the shale at his feet, then pushed himself clear and turned, a soft, sweatsoaked grin cracking his face.

'Figured yuh'd break from the others,' he drawled. 'Huckerman style, ain't it? Always the loner when it came to it.' He spat into the rocks. 'That how it was when yuh did for Frank? Just you and him?'

'Just like that,' said Tom, his gaze tight and fixed, 'save that Frank threw down his gun and pleaded to live. Would've mebbe let him too, hadn't been for the other piece he'd got hidden. Rat nearly took me out with that. Dealin' from the bottom seems to run in the family.'

Coyne's grin gleamed through his sweat. 'So there ain't no point in talkin' this through?'

'None,' grunted Tom. 'Yuh should've done yuh worst back there in Morton when yuh had yuh chance.'

'Yuh goin' to pull that trigger there, no messin'?'

'Yuh readin' it right, Scaffs. Time this was finished. I just ain't for havin' yuh on my tail. Yuh get it?'

'I get it.' The grin faded as Coyne scuffed a boot through the shale. ' 'Course, this ain't Pickford, is it, and I ain't Frank? Yuh should think about that, Huckerman. Me, I got my own way of doin' things. Take this situation for an instance — '

Coyne's sudden lunge for the boulders broke Tom's concentration as the loose, easy limbs and body facing him flashed into life and movement like an explosion. He dropped to one knee, a Colt already tight and levelled, and cursed through a hissing breath, but probed the piece too late for a shot at the disappearing legs and butt as Coyne buried himself behind the rock mound.

'Sonofabitch,' he hissed again, scrambling now for whatever slim cover of shadow he could find, then blinked and swished the sweat from his face in the rush of breaking light. Hell, he was a barn-door-size target out here if Coyne got to taking him on. All the fellow had to do was slip a barrel between the boulders. One shot, a split-second of searing lead . . .

Tom slithered to his knees, lost his balance, at the ominous, echoing crunch of splitting rock ahead of him. He grabbed wildly for a hold, fingers sliding like aimless roots through loose stones, and blinked furiously at the sight of the already shifting bulk of the boulder.

It was going to topple, damn it!

Coyne's desperation, the sheer will of strength, had finally cracked the mound. Now it would need no more than one last heave to send the mass crashing to the track below, a whole frenzied avalanche tumbling in its wake, clear into the path of Ed and the women — with no place for them to escape to and about as much chance of finding one as lifting a snowflake out of sunlight.

19

'Get the hell out of it! Get clear!'

Tom's screamed warning cracked over the morning silence with all the suddenness and urgency of the shots that blazed from his Colt only seconds later as he scrambled towards the rocking boulder.

No sign of Coyne now, but he was there, sure enough, straining his guts fit to burst far side of the mound for the final push. And he was going to make it! No stopping him. No target to shoot at. No hold on the rocks.

The sweat spun from Tom's brow, soaked into his shirt as he struggled higher. Had Ed heard the shots? Damn it, he must have. Fellow was not deaf. But would he react, or reckon the blaze for being aimed at Coyne?

'Get the hell out!'

The shout sounded empty, hollow,

crumbling out of Tom's throat as uselessly as the slithering stones at his feet. He hissed a curse, fired another shot, this time aimed at the mound, lost his footing for a moment but scrambled on, within only feet now of the perilously perched boulder.

It was going — groaning, splintering, the first loose rocks already skidding from sight towards the trail. One last push, damn it, just one more effort. But that would leave Coyne exposed. That would be the moment of the reckoning when the first fast shot from the steadiest Colt would be the end of it. No stopping the boulder, but wherever it was going, Scaffs Coyne would be right behind it.

Tom launched himself forward again, his Colt in a tighter grip, blood racing, heart pounding, sweat spinning. Coyne had been right, he thought, this was not Pickford, nothing like it, not one bit, but the outcome was hell-bent for being much the same — it would close in a killing.

He had come to within barely a hand's reach of the mound when the boulder finally split from its perch with a shuddering groan, hovered like some hulk of a bird feeling for its wings, and crashed to the slope. A dust-cloud rose blinding Tom's view of where he was scrambling to and just where Coyne would be when it cleared.

'Goddamn sonofabitch!' he cursed, spitting dust, blinking, then tripping headlong across Coyne's legs.

The thud of body to body sent Tom's Colt spinning from his grip, toppled Coyne from his balance and launched the two men into the tide of rocks rushing in the wake of the bouncing boulder.

Coyne's groans and shouts were drowned in the race of stone. Tom Huckerman slithered and slid on his back, a helpless twist of arms and legs. He bumped across Coyne's knees, caught the full force of a boot in his ribs, reached wildly for a hold but grabbed only space, choked on flying dirt, winced at the piercing thrust of a rock across his midriff and was tasting warm, fresh blood as a flurry of limbs tangled with his own.

The snorts of panicking horses, clatter of hoofs, Ed Wood's shouted but inaudible orders to the screaming women, added to the crazed, bewildering sounds that had shaken the morning into mayhem.

How far now to the track, wondered Tom; would his body stay in one piece or would he find himself buried in a coffin of rock, Coyne breathing his last at his side?

Had Ed escaped with the women?

Would the darkness close in on a fleeting image of Holly?

They were still falling, still slithering as useless as dirt on a wild night wind, still locking, unlocking in a frenzy of flailing limbs. Only once in those shuddering minutes had Tom glimpsed Coyne's dust-smeared face, a grey mask with twisted lips and gleaming eyes, but that had been enough: Pickford was alive and seething right there in the mocking stare.

'Damn yuh, Huckerman, I'll see yuh in Hell!' growled Coyne as he lashed a boot into Tom's thigh.

'Don't bank on it!' groaned Tom, as he rolled again through another mass of tumbling rocks and swirling dirt.

But it was then, as the roll bounced him into a face-down slither, that he felt the reassuring bulk of the still holstered twin Colt. His fingers clawed instinctively for a hold on the butt, touched it, lost it in the racing slither. Damn it, what the hell use was a gun strapped to a fellow's side if he could not reach it?

And then, in a sudden final flurry, clouds of dust and almost ear-splitting lessening of sound as the boulder split and crashed to a fragmented rest and the following sea of loose rocks cracked to a halt, he was there, flat on his back on the track.

Tom spat dirt and rubbed his knuckles into his eyes as he struggled to his feet, his dust-washed gaze searching frantically for the bulk of Coyne. He heard the snorts of horses, more distant now, another bellowing shout from Ed Woods, but nothing of the women, and was staggering forward, the Colt drawn, when a hissing growl spun him round to his left.

Coyne was already fully upright and rushing towards him like a demented animal, his clothes torn and ripped, face and neck blood-smeared, arms reaching, fingers spread, his growls frothing saliva at his lips, the sweat spinning from him.

'To hell with you, Tom Huckerman,' he bellowed. 'Go rot in it!'

Tom braced himself where he stood, his gaze steady now, the Colt easy in his grip, the taste of his own blood bitter and sticky on his cut lips.

'Not this day, Coyne,' he murmured as the man pounded on. 'I got other concerns and places to be, and this ain't it.'

He waited until it seemed that Coyne had only to crash a few more steps to smother him like a scudding shadow before levelling the Colt at his hip, steadying the hold, narrowing his gaze, taking the pressure that would unleash the blaze.

The lead spat like a tongue through the drifting dust, buried itself in Coyne, spun him to left and right as his eyes widened, fiery as the sunlight, and sent him toppling headlong into the rocks.

Tom swallowed long and deep and did not shift his gaze from the body for a full minute.

He had seen the last of Pickford.

★　★　★

The silence was back, the dust hanging like a veil of old breath, the sun glare settling to a shimmer, when Dori Maguire, Perdy, Ed Woods and the weary, sweat lathered mounts shuffled slowly and without a word to Tom's side.

Nobody spoke until their long stares had taken in the sprawled body of

Coyne and then flicked nervously to the face of the man who had shot him.

'Had that comin' from way back, I guess,' spat Ed, wiping a rag across his neck. 'Sonofabitch!'

'Yuh can say that again,' said Dori, shrugging her shoulders beneath the poncho. 'Reckoned us for bein' buried alive back there. Hell, hadn't been for them warnin' shots . . . ' She hesitated and moved closer to Tom. 'Damn it, mister, yuh all in there. As if bein' pinned under that rafter weren't enough — '

'We need to hole-up some place,' snapped Ed. 'Need time, get to thinkin' things through. Food, water . . . And some sleep, f'Crissake!'

'Sleep all yuh want, rest as long as it takes,' said Tom hoarsely, as he turned, his wet, red-rimmed eyes piercing like flints. 'We water the mounts and yuh catch up with me when yuh good and ready.'

'In God's name, Tom, y'self more than any of us needs to rest.'

'Yuh heard me, Ed. This ain't the place for chewin' over old cud. We been through that.'

'Now you fellas hold it right there,' bristled Dori, swishing a cloud of dust from the folds of the poncho. 'Ease up, will yuh? Damn it, you'd have yuh blood boilin' fit to choke yuh carry on like this. Ain't doin' nobody no good, 'specially that young gal out there — wherever she is.' She paused, conscious of Tom's gaze tight on her face. 'We ain't goin' no place, are we,' she went on firmly but carefully, 'not without we get to figurin' it? And before yuh say it, mister, that don't mean sittin' warmin' our butts in soft sand. I ain't for that. Same goes for Perdy here. All of us. But, hell, we get to splittin' up after this' — she gestured to the dead body — 'and all we been through, don't make no sense.'

'She's right, Tom,' murmured Ed.

' 'Course I'm right!' said Dori through the softest grin. 'Not every time — hell, no — but I am over this.'

Tom slid his exhausted, dirt-scuffed weight to one hip. 'So what yuh sayin' there, ma'am?' he asked.

Dori swished the poncho again. 'I figure it like this: them scumbags holdin' yuh gal ain't got nowhere to go save deeper into these Godforsaken mountains. Don't ask me why or where they got in mind, but they're here, you bet. Somewhere, goin' some place they know to. So we just keep followin', holdin to the trail best we can. Watching, listening, waiting, if we have to. Time'll come . . . Well, mebbe it will, mebbe it won't. That ain't for us to know. Not yet.'

'Why yuh doin' this?' said Tom, his gaze narrowing. 'Why any of yuh doin' it? Yuh ain't no good cause.'

'If yuh don't know now, mister, yuh ain't never goin' to,' clipped Dori. 'And besides, way yuh been handlin' them guns, we ain't for rubbin' yuh up rough. Gets kinda scary! All right? So shall we cut the cacklin' and get movin'?'

Perdy shifted uneasily to Dori's side. Ed Woods began to sweat. Tom Huckerman merely grunted.

And the morning sun rose higher, hot and staring.

20

Every sound a curse, every shadow a threat; pitch the two together in the haunting bleakness of the Broken Necks and a fellow, any fellow, woman along of him, had all the prospect of a lousy, sweat-soaked day.

It was that, sure enough, thought Ed, bringing up the rear of the trailing mounts on the winding, rock-strewn track, and would maybe get a whole lot worse before another night closed in. Damn it, who could say what the next shadow might be hiding? Who was to know what lurked back of the sounds out there that echoed like a whisper? Could be they were being watched right now. And could be the eyes were settled smooth as a rattler's gaze down the gleaming barrel of a Winchester.

Not a body here who would really know, not for certain, he reckoned.

Dori Maguire was smart, could handle herself with a whip-stinging tongue, but that was all saloon and bedroom talk. Things were a whole lot different out here. Talk did not stop bullets, and mountains were no bedroom. Same went for young Perdy, who was gut-scared anyhow.

Tom Huckerman had an edge, sure enough, keen as a honed blade, and a resolve as fixed as the peaks up there, but, hell, he was physically near washed up. However the fallen rafter had left him, the showdown with Coyne had deepened it. Might only be a question of time — on a short fuse at that — before he toppled from that mount out of sheer exhaustion. As for his speed with his fancy Colts, the sharp-shooting Mr Huckerman might be counting himself lucky to be clearing leather come sundown.

Which brought him none too comfortably to himself.

Hell, he was tired! Law-making in the soft underbelly of a quiet plains' town was no experience for hot hoofing it in pursuit of scumbag kidnappers. Not at his age! Another day, if he made it that far, and he would be happy enough to sleep where he dropped — assuming he had the strength to drop. And then, there was this place, the mountains, the stifling heat, the endless track to maybe nowhere and certainly the unknown.

Yessir, just as he had been reckoning miles back, all the prospect of a lousy, sweat-soaked day! No figuring it other, not unless . . .

Tom had reined up, slid from his mount and crunched anxiously into a clearing between a stand of boulders, Dori Maguire following in his steps.

'What yuh got there?' called Ed. 'Yuh seen somethin'?'

'You bet,' said Dori. 'They been here, and not long back.'

Tom Huckerman was moving round the edge of the clearing like an animal skulking at the lair of its prey as Ed came to Dori's side.

'See that?' she murmured softly.

'Ashes. Day old, I'd reckon. Footprints, hoof scuffs. I'd figure the scumbags holin' up here for the night. But, hell,' she sighed, 'just where they headin'? Can't be a deal between here and the border, and then nothin' when yuh get there.'

They watched Tom's slow, measured steps in silence, neither wanting, or daring, to break the agony of his thoughts as his gaze probed and shifted over every sliver of ash, every print, mark, stone and rock.

'He figurin' on findin' somethin' of the gal?' whispered Ed.

'Wouldn't you in his boots?' said Dori.

Ed swallowed, wiped a hand across the sweat in his neck and eased his aching body into a patch of shade.

'One thing's for sure,' said Dori, her gaze still following Tom, 'we ain't so far out in our reckonin'. No doubtin' them fellas are goin' deeper. Just wish we knew how deep and just where — '

'The camp. It's gotta be the camp.'

Three pairs of eyes flicked to Perdy where she sat her mount on the track.

'What's that?' frowned Dori. 'Camp? What camp?'

'I heard a fella talk of it back there at Brenard's. Some sorta minin' camp.'

'Minin'?' croaked Ed. 'Damnit, there ain't been nothin' worth liftin' a pick for in these parts for years.'

'Could've been way back,' said Dori. 'Yuh sure about this, Perdy?'

'Just got to recallin' it and only heard talk of the place one time. Fella passin' through like the rest said as how he'd come from the camp. Never saw him again.'

'When?' snapped Tom, his gaze intense and gleaming. 'When did this fella pass through?'

Perdy shrugged. 'Months back. Snow was still lyin'.'

'He alone?'

'Just him. Quiet sort. Never said no more as I recall.'

'Talk was out East as how they mined for silver hereabouts,' said Ed. 'Never came to much. Just scratchin's. But, hell, that was before I got my badge. Lifetime ago.'

'Supposin' somebody got to scratchin' again,' murmured Dori. 'Supposin' they're still here. Could be, and could be them scumbags know of 'em. If the mine's been opened up and there's fellas out here, it's just the sorta place to . . . ' She hesitated, her fingers fumbling nervously at the poncho. 'What I mean to say is — '

'I'll say it for yuh, ma'am,' croaked Tom. 'Just the sorta place to sell a young gal.'

'Chances are, o'course — ' began Dori again.

'We're wastin' time,' said Tom, crossing from the clearing to his mount. 'I wanna be spittin' on that camp before sundown.'

Ed Woods swallowed on a long, silent groan. He had a notion, clear as this scorched, baking day, that a lousy, sweat-soaked night was coming up fast.

*　★　★*

The hours dragged mercilessly for the four riders as they made their way ever deeper into the heart of the Broken Necks on that airless, soundless day.

Noon came and went under the blaze of a high sun bathing the track in a shimmering glare of heat where even the shade held little cool comfort for bodies already stretched to the limit and lathered in the pinch of sweat.

And if the heat and haunting silence of the trail were not enough to drain the riders of clear thinking, their jumbled thoughts of when, where and how that day might end brought their own agony.

Dori Maguire's mind swirled with images of a life spent measuring every hour of every day and night against the odds of survival, and wondering now if in trailing back of a fellow with only one resolve to settle, at any price, Fate

217

had dealt her the last dud card.

Only trouble was, the slick-shooting, one-time gunslinger was just about the first fellow she had crossed whose eyes had not done the undressing at a first glance. And now, damn it, she might not live long enough to enjoy it. Story of her life. But, hell, the last chapter might take some beating!

Perdy, following short of Dori, was confused, in one breath rejoicing at her escape from Brenard's, in the next wondering if she would ever pass beyond the Broken Necks again, save slung limp on a pack mount.

Even so, Tom Huckerman was right to be set as determined as he was, and she for one would be along of him till that gal of his was . . . She cared not to dwell too long on that score. After all, she had been there, seen it, known it, but there had been no pa trailing out for her.

Ed Woods was not only melting physically, his brain was fast turning to sponge.

So what if there was a long forgotten mining camp buried deep in these bone-dry, dust-wasted hills, and supposing it had been opened up again by some half-starved no-hopers riding their luck? Sure, the luckless scratchers would welcome the Trulso raiders and their prize with open arms, and pay well enough for the privileges, but where did that leave Tom Huckerman, a middle-aged lawman and two women in the chances of rescuing the girl? Damnit, there could be as many as a dozen, fifteen, maybe more guns ranged against them, and not even Huckerman, fast as he might be, could face odds stacked that high and stay dealing at an even table.

Best he could hope for was the satisfaction of having made the effort and some sonofabitch being sober enough to steady his aim. Same could be said for all of them, the women especially.

But, then, supposing there was no camp, or no more than the dead, rotting shell of one long abandoned? What then? Just how far, and for how long, did Tom plan to trail the raiders? From here to the border and beyond, while ever there was land to cross and a new horizon to reach?

More to the point in that case, who among them would be ready and willing enough to pack a lifetime into Tom Huckerman's saddle-bags? Now that might take a deal more thinking through than simply reining a mount's head to the next trail.

It was one thing to stand to a fellow in his need, but it was sure as hell something else to expect . . .

Smoke, the first drifting hint of it two miles on where the trail skirted the ridge to a drop that might be a sprawling canyon below the northern peaks.

So there was a camp, thought Ed, reining alongside the others as they halted to gaze at the curling twist. Sure there was, but had it been the final destination of the raiders? Were they still there? And just where and in what state was Holly Huckerman?

'We close in come dusk,' murmured Tom, his fingers turning the crucifix at his sweat-lathered neck.

21

'Not a hope, and yuh'd be half crazy to think there was. It'd be no better than walkin' to a slaughterhouse.' Ed Woods croaked the words over the stiff dusk air, blinked his tired eyes on the fading light and eased away from the brim of the ridge. 'We're goin' to have to think again, Tom. Ain't nothin' else for it.'

He winced at the throb of his aching limbs and lay still and relaxed for a moment on the cooler surface of the rock slab. Give him a minute, maybe less, and he would be sleeping the sleep of the exhausted. Give him ten and he might never get to waking. He blinked again and slid a slow gaze to where Tom Huckerman lay tense and concentrated at his side. How come this fellow never got to looking even worn? Hardly surprising he had weathered out the life back there on the Trulso plain.

'Well,' croaked Ed again, gritting his teeth on another throb, 'what yuh reckon? Don't look good, does it? There's bodies down there in that tumbledown shack, sure enough, but a darn sight too many for us to take on. Wouldn't get to seein' the size of their boots, let alone — '

'A dozen,' hissed Tom, his eyes narrowing to dark tight slits. 'Twelve at most, includin' them scumbag raiders. Yuh can count the mounts back of that lean-to.'

'Yeah, OK, so there's twelve of 'em,' sighed Ed. 'Ten too many by my reckonin', shape we're in. No chance of drawin' fire power, not just the two of us.'

'And Holly. She's there. Just know she is.'

'Now hold on there, Tom,' said Ed, easing a gentle hand to Tom's arm. 'Yuh can't be certain. Ain't nothin' yuh can see from here to say she is. Place is just four walls, a roof, windows, door and a curl of smoke. Sure, there's horses and there ain't no doubtin' who's been saddled up on some of 'em, but that still ain't to say as how Holly's . . . ' He swallowed on a dust-pinched throat. 'Hell, Tom, there ain't nobody willin' that gal to be alive more than me. I'd give my eye-teeth to see her smilin' face again, but we gotta reckon the facts: even if Holly is alive, and God willin' that's so, we ain't got a sniff of a hope of gettin' to her, have we, not ranged against guns like them rats'll be sproutin'?

'And look at the distance 'tween us here and them down there; quarter-mile if it's a spit, and not one mangy scrap of cover across an inch of it. There'd be Colts, Winchesters, and a whole darned armoury pinnin' us minute we put boot to dirt. Them raiders'd recognize yuh straight off, Tom, and yuh can bet yuh pants them minin' fellas ain't exactly strainin' for company.' Ed paused and swallowed again. 'I ain't for seein' yuh dead, not no way, I ain't — and I ain't for joinin' yuh neither!'

'Didn't invite yuh,' murmured Tom.

'So yuh didn't, but yuh sure as hell got me, same as yuh have them women waitin' there back of yuh. Yuh got the whole dirt-caked heap of us, Tom, and we ain't for goin' nowheres. But that ain't to say we've given up. Hell, no! We come this far and we're standin' to yuh — but that's it, ain't it, we gotta stay standin'? Ain't a clap of use to yuh gal there flat on our backs.'

A line of sweat beaded bright and wet on Tom's brow. 'I'm goin' in, Ed. I ain't got no choice,' he whispered.

'Sure,' soothed Ed, 'sure yuh are, but let's figure on levellin' the odds, shall we? Give me a coupla days and I could mebbe have ten fellas standin' to us. Must be somebody, some place hereabouts — '

'That's whistlin' on a plain's wind, Ed, and yuh know it. I doubt there's another livin' soul in fifty miles, and I ain't got the time for waitin' on findin' out.' Tom licked his lips and narrowed his eyes again. 'I'm goin' in at full dark,' he said.

'Of all the mule heads,' groaned Ed, wincing as his body tensed, 'if yuh ain't the dumbest — '

'Yuh heard me. Get y'self and the women clear. Ain't no call for spillin' blood unnecessary.'

'Unnecessary, f'Crissake! *Unnecessary?* Well, now, ain't that just generous of yuh! Hell, I'd figure a gesture like that for bein' real grand! Sure, I would. Why I ain't crossed nothin' so generous since — '

Ed choked on his words at the sound of a soft scuffling at the foot of the rock slab.

'You two all through spittin' at each other, or can anyone join in?'

'Help y'self,' grunted Ed as he squirmed clear of Tom and slid to Dori Maguire's side in the shadowed cleft of the rocks. 'Fella ain't thinkin' straight.'

'I heard,' said Dori, settling her hands on her hips beneath the poncho, her piercing gaze tight on Tom's sprawled body above her. 'Can't say I blame yuh, mister, but yuh ain't figurin' it for real, pair of yuh.'

Ed sighed and wiped a hand over his aching eyes. 'And I suppose you are? Yuh got the whole situation panned out and simple as handin' out candy to kids. Tell me!'

'Ain't no call for bein' whippy-tongued, Mr Woods,' said Dori quietly, her stare burning like a light over Ed's face. 'I ain't for bein' talked down to. Don't become a man of the law. But, yeah, me and Perdy here been sortin' things through and, sure, we got some notion what we might do — 'bout all we *can* do when yuh get to it. Nothin' brilliant, but like Mr Huckerman there is fond of puttin' it, it's as good as we got right now.'

'And?' murmured Ed.

'Two things we don't know,' said Dori, folding her arms with a flourish of the poncho. 'We can't be certain the gal is still with them scum raiders down there. Chances are she is, but we gotta be sure, and we gotta know *where* she is and in what sorta condition. Gettin' her outa that camp alive and in one piece is all that counts. Foul up and we could good as finish her. Two, we don't know how many fellas holed-up in that rats' nest. Five raiders we know to, but how many more, who are they and what sorta mood they in? I can guess — can I just! — but we gotta be certain before we get to any hell-raisin'.'

Dori paused, her gaze unblinking into Ed's eyes, and went on, 'Ask y'self who can ride into that minin' dump there and pass right through the door like it was home from home, and yuh got only one answer.'

'Now hold it right there,' spluttered Ed. 'If you think for one minute — '

'I'd figure them fellas there for bein' wound up fit to burst a gut,' snapped Dori, dismissing Ed's splutter. 'Me and Perdy ridin' in tame as lambs is goin' to seem like they struck a whole river of silver, 'specially when they know we're one-time Brenard's gals on the loose.

Give us an hour, two at most, and Perdy and me'll have 'em eatin' out of our hands like they were babes. Then all we gotta do — '

'That is just about the craziest, dumbest thing I ever heard,' spluttered Ed again. 'Damnit, I'd sooner — '

'Yuh got any doubts, Sheriff, why don't yuh ask the fella there? Ask him if this ain't the only way we got of gettin' that gal of his outa the hole she's in. Ask him — right now while we still got time, before it's too damn late and we're all waitin' on bein' crow meat.'

★   ★   ★

'Yuh could get to starin' Hell face-on for this, Tom Huckerman,' groaned Ed — squirming another few inches higher to the very rim of the ridge overlooking the shadowed sprawl of the canyon below. He settled himself, narrowed his gaze on the brooding bulk of the lantern-lit mining shack, then glanced quickly at the man pressed tight to the rocks as his side. 'But I guess yuh already know that,' he murmured.

'I know it,' said Tom, without shifting his stare. 'T'ain't nothin' I ain't used to.'

'But, damnit, Tom, them women are as good as signin' their own death warrants down there. Minute they're spotted and one of them scum steps outside that shack, they can start countin' to their last breath, and it ain't goin' to come easy neither. Yuh got any idea of what they're facin'?'

'Don't need tellin'. Neither do they.'

'But yuh let 'em go just the same. Didn't hear yuh protestin' none. Didn't hear yuh sayin' as how there might be another way. Hell, we could've *found* another way, couldn't we?'

'Could we?' said Tom. 'Dori didn't figure so — and before yuh say it again, she ain't goin' to die, neither her nor Perdy. I ain't goin' to let 'em. Yuh can rest easy on that.'

'Rest easy, f'Crissake!' croaked Ed,

beginning to sweat in spite of the cooler night air. 'Mister, I ain't been restin' nothin' like easy in days, and now ain't the time for gettin' started.' He grunted again and fell silent as he scanned the canyon. 'Hard to see anythin' down there, damnit,' he grated through clenched teeth. 'Yuh see anythin'?'

'They just cleared the rocks to yuh right, Dori leadin', Perdy bringin' up the pack horse. Five minutes and they'll be spotted.'

'That's for sure,' moaned Ed. 'And then what? We just goin' to lie out here like lizards?'

'Just that,' murmured Tom.

'Hell, this is goin' to be some night! Mebbe we should get closer.'

'No,' snapped Tom, 'we don't do nothin'. Leave it to Dori. She'll know what to do and when to do it. And she'll be reckonin' on us for watchin'.'

Ed Woods eased a hot, sticky, stubble-scratched cheek to the rock face and swallowed on a throat as sharp as crushed stone. 'Just hope they find . . . ' he began, but thought better of it.

A silent prayer seemed more in keeping.

22

Sizzling slices of thick, lean ham and fried eggs coming sunnyside up in a pan as round and dark as . . . Cloud scudding deep and fast across the moon.

Ed twitched out of sleep as if prodded with a hot poker, blinked and slid a near numb hand over the rock slab. Hell, he thought, twitching again at the lathering of cold sweat coating his limbs, he had slid away there for a minute, lost himself in a fevered sleep. Must have got to dreaming some.

He ran an acid tongue over dry lips and glanced quickly for the shape of Tom at his side. Still there, thank God, still wide awake and watching, eyes bright as a hungry hawk, fingers clenched tight on the rim of the ridge.

'What's happenin'?' he croaked.

'Nothin',' hissed Tom through no

more than a weary blink of heavy lids. 'Women are in the shack. Ain't been a sound since. Only one light now far end.'

'Hell!' spat Ed, rolling to his stomach, and peering into the canyon. 'Anything could've happened. Supposin' them rats — '

'No time for supposin', Ed,' clipped Tom. 'Time to shift.'

'We goin' down there?'

'*I'm* going down there. Take advantage of this clouded moon. Make for them rocks to yuh left. Goin' to be outa sight for a while, so you keep yuh eyes on that shack. Join me when I signal. Got it?'

'I got it,' sighed Ed. 'But I sure as hell don't like it.'

'Nothin' about any of this to like, Ed. We ain't in the likin' business. Not a deal of choosin' neither. Just doin'.'

'So it seems,' muttered Ed as he watched Tom slide from the rock slab and slip silently into the deeper night. 'Yeah, just that.'

Tom waited, took a deep breath, shrugged his shoulders against the stiffness, ran his hands over his aching legs, watched and listened for a moment, then moved.

The going from the rock slab over the first of the drop to the floor of the canyon came easy; firm ground, tight rocks, a track that could be measured against fast but careful steps through a darkness broken only intermittently by the shift of cloud across the high yellow moon.

How long to a hint of dawn, he wondered; how best to use the hours of night, and what then? What had Dori and Perdy found in the shack? Had they come this far only to discover it all a waste?

He halted and shuddered. No point in thinking the worst, scant comfort right now in praying for the best. There was too much at stake, lives already hanging by the thinnest of threads, including his own. He tapped the butts of his Colts, took another deep breath, and moved on.

Firm ground gave way to shale, loose stone, trickling ankle-deep sand, then, almost without warning, as if a clenched fist had opened suddenly to a flat hand, he was into the open and shafting stabs of moonlight as the cloud cover cleared.

He scurried like some startled beetle for a line of low rock and fell flat on his stomach behind it.

'Easy, easy,' he murmured, spitting grit from his teeth, swallowing on a throat as parched as bleached hide. He waited, blinking on the pitch of the dark, listening for sounds. Nothing save the whisperings of night, the distant snort of a mount loose-hitched at the shack.

Just what in hell was going on in there, he wondered, or did he need to ask? Maybe he could already imagine, see it like the flickerings of bleak nightmare: the scheming defiance in

Dori Maguire's eyes, the despairing fear in Perdy's, and somewhere, lost in shadow, the face of a girl who no longer saw anything and felt only dread.

He shivered, licked his lips and raised his head slowly above the rock line.

Still only the faint glow from a single lantern at the shack; no sounds, no movements. His gaze shifted to the steeper, thicker bulge of rocks Ed Woods would be watching for his signal. A few fast strides and he would be there, that much closer to the shack, almost within spitting distance of the tumbledown timbers, rotting lean-to and veranda, cracked, cobwebbed windows and the door that leaned on its hinges like a drunk and would groan like one at a touch.

Place looked as if it would fall apart if a fellow so much as coughed, he thought, but it was not the place that mattered, was it? Hell, no, it was the scum it was harbouring. A dozen and maybe more guns and not one of them a mite fussed about its target, not out here in a Godforsaken wilderness where life passed for no more than the dirt it stood in.

He blinked, glanced quickly to the smudge of the rock slab high above him, came slowly to his knees then his feet and, without daring to think twice about it, ran for the bulge.

He was there and deep behind it in seconds.

Wait, give it time for the ache in his legs to ease, catch his breath, take stock of where he was, what he could see. Damn, he could hear, sure enough, loud and clear: the shack door groaning open, creaking, scraping across the veranda boards; then the slurred, dull thud of boots, wheezing cough, croaked curse, swish of spittle.

Silence.

Tom waited, stiff and tense, eyes wide in one moment, narrowed in a concentration of senses in the next, hardly daring to so much as swallow.

Footfalls now. Somebody walking the veranda, passing from the lantern glow to the shadowed end. Coming Tom's way. Pausing. More coughing, more spittle. A yawn. A waft of fetid, liquored breath. Three more steps. Tap of a tired boot. Another step, two, closer, still closer.

Then nothing.

Fellow must have stepped from the veranda to the sand, thought Tom, lifting a slow, careful hand to wipe the cold sweat from his cheek. Hell, he could be anywhere, going anywhere!

Tom eased his weight across the bulk of the rocks towards a narrow crevice to the sand line. Keep it steady, keep it easy, he told himself, blinking on more sweat. Fellow out there figured on having the night to himself.

Pause, concentrate, listen.

Scuff of boots through sand. The sound of heavy breathing. Smell of stale mescal and cigar smoke.

And then the sudden looming of the shadow, long and lean across the sand. Moving on, waiting. Fellow had turned to gaze at the moon, maybe reckoning on another hot day coming up; taking in the fresher air, wondering if he should get back to the shack, have himself a woman again while the going was better than it had been in months.

Stay moon-struck, thought Tom, as he pushed himself clear of the rock, gritted his teeth, eased a Colt clear of leather, and shifted like another stab of the light.

He was at the man's back in three fast strides, the barrel of the gun already cleaving air for the fellow's head. Tom felt the thud, heard the soft groan, a gurgling in the man's throat, and was dragging the limp body into cover in seconds.

He slid the Colt to its holster with a grunt and stared into the lifeless face at his feet. Not one of the raiders, that was for sure, but not a whisker short of the scum. Probably had them filthy fingers . . .

He stiffened again at the drift of another shadow, smaller, softer, hesitant — damn it, moving into the rocks!

'Perdy? That you?'

The girl shivered and stifled a croak. 'Dori said . . . said as how,' she stammered, 'to . . . to get out here, see if yuh had moved in.'

'What yuh seen?' hissed Tom anxiously, the sweat standing like pebbles on his brow. 'Is — ?'

'Yuh gal's here, mister. Bad shape, but she's alive. Dori said — '

'Get back!' hissed Tom again at the sound of the shack door groaning open, the thud of more boots. 'Get back, yuh hear? I'm comin' for yuh soon as I can.'

'Noon,' croaked Perdy already easing back to the veranda. 'Them raiders are pullin' out at noon. Be here!'

★ ★ ★

'Hell, this is no better than sittin' over an open fire with yuh butt scorchin' and yuh feet in boilin' water!'

Ed Woods shifted in the sand like an irritable lizard, glanced at the still lifeless body of the miner, then, with a

241

quick lick of his lips and a fast hand over his dirt and sweat-matted stubble, at the silent, staring shape of Tom Huckerman crouched a yard or so distant.

Fellow sure looked to be in a turmoil, he thought, wincing as he swallowed; torn between a flood of elation at the news of Holly, but damned to wait, about as impotent as a sliver of rock, till at least first light and maybe a deal longer. And meantime, his mind crowded fit to burst to a fury.

'What yuh figurin', Tom?' he asked. 'We goin' to sit it out? Noon sure as hell seems like a year away. Ain't no sayin' neither as how we won't be spotted long before. Them rats'll come up for air soon as there's a wink of light. Wouldn't give a spit for our chances then, not this close. Maybe we should pull back again, eh, get ourselves into the hills? What yuh reckon?'

'I reckon we stay,' murmured Tom. 'We do as Perdy said: be here.'

'Sure, sure,' soothed Ed, flexing his stiffening shoulders, 'we'll be here. No question, but we're a dumb-dead target at this range, ain't we? Just the two of us and a heap of rocks. Ain't much of an edge. Anythin' more than three guns pulled on us and we'll be cold meat.'

'Yuh f'gettin' Dori. She ain't goin' to be sittin' prim as a schoolma'am.'

'Mebbe not, but she ain't goin' to be no ragin' gunslinger in there neither. Assumin' she can get to a gun. Me, I'm all for puttin' this scumbag here to permanent sleep and easin' away. Chances are — '

'Them horses there,' clipped Tom, nodding to the line of loose-hitched mounts. 'Ain't none of them fellas goin' no place without them. Yuh reckon? So what say we cut the hoofs from under the scum? Take 'em out, one by one, real soft, real quiet.'

'Hell, that's a darned sight easier in the sayin' than the doin'. Yuh goin' to have to shift like — '

'A shadow?' queried Tom. 'So cover me.'

★   ★   ★

It took Tom the far side of two long, sweating hours to clear the mounts from the hitch line; two hours of slipping softly, silently between the rock cover, the lean-to and the line like some huddled, haunting ghost shape that seemed never to be in one place for longer than a passing breath, that came, paused and went as if on a night breeze.

Ed watched from the rocks, Colt primed and heavy in his hand, his body and senses tensed to near splitting, from the edge of his teeth to the tips of his fingers, but strangely after an hour with growing confidence.

Damn it, he thought, the fellow was going to do it, shift the mounts with the calm and ease of a range hand tidying a cluttered corral. No hurry, no sweat — Ed was doing enough for both of them! — soothing each mount as he reached it, whispering deep into its ears, hands soft and gentle, and every movement measured against the need for calm.

Some one-time gunslinger, mused Ed! How many times had the fellow coaxed himself a means of escape from under the very noses of some dozing lawman?

So maybe he did get lucky when an old mare bucked a mite too sharp, but the sleeping fellows in the shack slept on, too liquored up and woman crazed to stir further than whatever dreams they clattered round.

Only once had Ed risked a closer gaze at one of the shack's cracked windows, wondering if maybe Dori and Perdy were aware of what was happening. Wondering too if the luck, if you could call it that from where they stood, would hold with them.

The light was already breaking, white and wide in the east, when Tom was done and he settled again at Ed's side. And there was nothing in the man's eyes then to tell of what was to come.

Not unless you stared long enough to see the steel.

23

'Yuh seen this, mister?' groaned Ed, his face gleaming under a lathering of clinging sweat. ' 'Cus if yuh ain't, yuh'd sure as hell best get to looking — real hard!'

Tom Huckerman eased himself higher in the rocks, blinked against the glare of the sun and narrowed his gaze on the shadow-blackened miners' shack. 'Well, now,' he murmured, 'ain't that just set them a quandary.'

'Quandary, f'Crissake!' hissed Ed, shaking the sweat from his cheeks. 'That what yuh call it? Well, I'll tell yuh just what *I* call it — I call it hell's teeth all set to get gnashing faster than you can draw breath. That's what *I* call it! And I ain't one given to exaggerating. Damn it, Tom, just look, will yuh? What yuh seeing? Same as me: a dozen fellas out there, meaner-lookin' bunch as yuh'll ever cross, and right now in a real mean mood, wondering just what in hell's happened to their one-time hitched mounts. T'ain't going to take 'em long to figure, is it? And there's five of the scum there — yuh spotted 'em? — who ain't a spit short of coming to some conclusions. Yuh following me, Tom?'

'I'm lookin',' quipped Tom.

'Good, 'cus when yuh got a minute yuh might then get to figuring just why it is there ain't been the pinch of a sight come sun-up of Dori and Perdy. And when yuh done that, yuh might get to tellin' me — '

'Hold it there, Ed,' said Tom, shifting again. 'Easy does it.'

'*Easy does it, f'Crissake!*'

'Them's the raiders, sure enough. I can good as smell 'em. They'll be the first to make a move.'

Ed ran a hand over his sodden face. 'Hell, does it matter who moves first? Fact is, it's goin' to take just minutes for whoever's movin' to move right this way!'

'And we'll be ready,' said Tom quietly.

Ed shuffled back and sighed wheezily. 'Oh, sure, 'course we'll be ready. Two shots, *if* we get lucky, and that'll be that.' He sighed again. 'I come this far, Tom,' he went on slowly, 'and I stood to yuh for what I believe to be right, and I'm thankin' whoever it is up there that yuh gal's alive — *and* I couldn't give a damn about yuh past — but I gotta real hankerin' for a future which right now is fast fadin'.'

'That fella I put to sleep still breathin'?' snapped Tom.

'No, he ain't,' croaked Ed. 'He's dead.'

'Nobody's missin' him. That figures. Too darned busy workin' out what to do next. Take a look.'

Ed eased back to the rocks, raised himself to an eye-level view of the shack and squinted on the shimmering heat-haze. 'Raiders standin' apart, lookin' this way; one of 'em pointin' north. They reckon on findin' a track, mebbe trailin' the loose mounts. 'Bout the only choice they got.' He shifted his gaze. 'Minin' fellas just standin' there mouthin',' he grunted. 'It's a powder keg, Tom. Somethin's goin' to blow.'

'But not yet,' murmured Tom. 'Not 'til them five get to walkin'.'

'Yuh ain't figurin', are yuh — '

'If they move in a line, concentrate yuh fire on the flanks. Leave the centre to me. And don't miss!'

'But what about the others? They ain't goin' to just stand there watchin', are they?'

'I hope not, Ed, I surely hope not. But that's somethin' somebody else is goin' to have to figure.'

★　★　★

It was another sweltering half-hour, with the sun climbing high to full noon, the heat-haze shimmering until it seemed the land was boiling, the air flat and lifeless, before Tom Huckerman stirred again, and then only to ease his body to a new position and clear the sweat from his face and neck.

He took his time and waited a long minute to the moment when he placed a gentle hand on the slumped shoulders of Ed Wood and stirred him from his heat-soaked doze.

'Darnit,' muttered Ed, but fell instantly silent again at Tom's warning gesture for quiet.

'Them scum are all packed for hard trackin',' he whispered. 'Overdone it a mite for the distance they're goin'!'

But there was no response from Ed. His throat was parched to a rag, his tongue a bulge of hot stone, and he cared not to think too hard about the rest of him. Being able to see and handle a Colt was as good as he could hope to get right now.

He rolled to his knees and dragged himself to Tom's side. 'They movin' yet?'

'Any minute. Yuh goin' to be able to

handle this?' asked Tom. 'Don't have to, yuh know. Yuh just stay low here, keep yuh head down — '

'Why don't yuh do the sane thing for once, mister, and save yuh goddamn breath for fightin'!'

Tom tensed, his sweat-sodden shirt suddenly cold and tight across his back, his eyes lit with a glare of resolve and defiance. He reached slowly, instinctively for the butt of a Colt, fingers relaxed but steady, as if the movement had a mind of its own.

'Here they come,' he drawled. 'Big fella centre is all mine.'

The five men had turned from the front of the shack and stepped into line across the sand like slivers of shadow pared from the shade; two fellows taller than the rest, a third shorter and leaner, the fourth with a casual, rolling gait, and the fifth, a stride ahead of the others, thicker, bulkier, with the brim of his hat tipped low across his brow to darken his face but not the keen, measured glint in his eyes.

Three packed their Colts slung loose; two cradled rifles in crooked, easy arms; all carried canteens, slim bed-rolls, and one what looked to be a heavier sack heaved across a shoulder. The five were dressed in a ragbag assortment of torn, dust-creased clothes; one wore odd boots, the others creaked and scuffed their steps in tired, down-at-heel leather. The rolling gait fellow was humming, his companions silent. All had the same look of cold bitterness on their sun-scabbed, craggy faces.

None, it seemed to Ed in his fixed gaze on them, had ever been truly born of a mother, but hatched in the pit of Hell.

'Sonsofallbitches!' he croaked and swallowed without feeling a thing.

Tom counted the men's strides like he was numbering hogs in a pen, just as he had the Ristoff boys at Stand Bluff, calm and cool as he had been riding with the Kavanagh bunch into Stony Creek; with that same, unblinking stare that had burnished his mark through Pickford, Clifton, Semblance, a stare that told nothing, said nothing and no man had ever read.

Then, as the men's shadows lengthened and the distant scuffing of steps drew closer in heavier, deeper thuds, his eyes narrowed, images of flame and pillage danced across his mind, sounds of roaring fire and a young girl's scream filled his head, voices came and went and lingered in echoes, the prophesy of destiny in the words of Maggie McHay, the whispered love of a dying wife, the call for help from a vanishing daughter.

'Let's do this t'gether, May,' he murmured. 'Just like we always did.'

Tom Huckerman's guns were blazing fast and level almost before he was fully upright. The rolling gait fellow screamed and spun back through the heat-haze with a ribbon of his own red blood spinning from his throat like a snake in a turmoil.

Ed's gun spat true and deadly, taking out a man with a rifle, then swinging through a flashing arc to settle on the second, the lead biting deep as the fellow fumbled too late and bewildered to retaliate.

Tom launched himself from the rocks, cleared them and was flat on his stomach as his Colts blazed again, this time shattering the chest of the tall man, throwing him high so that for one grotesque split-second the sun glare reduced his face to a transparent ball of mottled grey bone.

Tom rolled, kicked to his knees, saw Ed's shot bury itself deep in the short man's thigh. He watched the fellow grasp at the wound, saw the twist of agony in his sweating face, then settled his misery with a single shot clean through the middle of his forehead and turned like a twist of light for the dark-faced man.

The man stood face-on to Tom, a scowl twisted to a half-grin at his cracked, broken lips, his eyes wide and wet and fixed, like flat pools after rainfall.

'Yuh crazed dimwit!' he leered. 'Yuh should've died long back, mister, burned to hell in that torchin' we had. But it ain't too late. Nossir, it ain't never too late.'

But it was this time as Tom's Colts opened up in a surging roar of flame. 'Don't never waste words when bullets are talkin',' he yelled above the rip of the blaze. 'And don't never tangle with a Huckerman, either this side of Heaven or far side of Hell. Got it?'

The man went down in an oozing splurge of blood, fell to his knees, crawled a yard, lifted his eyes and mouthed his last: 'I'll see yuh right there, mister, whoever yuh are — in Hell, damn yuh!'

'Sure,' clipped Tom, 'but just don't never turn yuh back, and don't never mouth me!'

And then he fired again, rocking the man's head back until it seemed it would snap clean from his body.

'The shack, it's goin' up!'

Ed's shout spun Tom from the

blood-soaked body to the sight of a thickening cloud of smoke blurring the mound of the rotting timbers to a darkening smudge licked by ripping tongues of flame.

'Dori's set fire to the heap!' he croaked again, struggling from the rocks.

'Pin them miners down,' yelled Tom, already forcing his aching limbs to work him through the sand. 'Don't let nobody get to Holly, f'Crissake!'

Ed pounded on to the shack, but shuddered to his bones at the snorting roar of a Winchester loosing lead high into smoke and flames. 'What the hell!' he mouthed, as he tripped, gathered himself and squinted against the shimmering haze and heat of the fire.

Tom was weaving across the sand in a whirl of limbs, Colts clutched tight, swirls of sweat spinning from his face, his whole body, it seemed, thrusting forward like some dark propelled mound of stone.

The miners, still confused and

reeling in bewilderment from the surprise attack and massacre of the raiders, had turned their wild, wide gazes from blood to flame as the fire gathered strength and devoured the roof of the shack in one roaring gulp and raced on hungry for more.

Ed staggered, cursed, blinked furiously, squirmed at the wash of the sweat in his neck, fell forward and collapsed to his knees. 'If this ain't just the craziest day I ever seen!' His dirt-streaked face cracked to a smile as Dori Maguire, Perdy at her side, loosed another round of shots over the miners' heads from the Winchester tight in her grip.

'Don't none of you scum so much as think of movin',' she bellowed, swinging the barrel across the line of men. 'Yuh stinkin' hole's goin' down to ash, and I ain't one bit sorry, and yuh'll be joinin' it faster than them flames there first one as steps a grain of sand closer. Now get back, lot of yuh. Get back and give that fella out there some breathin' space.

Yuh hear — back!'

Ed's gaze turned slowly to the open ground beyond the lean-to. 'You bet it's just one helluva day!' he croaked and smiled again as he watched Tom Huckerman drag himself through painful, scuffing steps to where his daughter waited in the sun's full glare, draw her to him and fold his arms around her. 'Yeah, one helluva day!'

★　★　★

'Ain't that just a sight for yuh sand-sore eyes?' smiled Dori, lifting the barrel of the rifle a fraction higher, her gaze flicking quickly from the sour-faced miners to Tom and the girl still locked in each other's arms. 'Worth every miserable mile of these goddamn mountains. What yuh reckon, Sheriff?'

'Sure,' murmured Ed, wiping more sweat from his neck, 'and I'm a deal taken with the sight of that Winchester there. Just how'd yuh get yuh hands on that, and how — ?'

259

'Whoa! Ease up there,' said Dori, with another lift of the barrel. 'Yuh know better than to ask gals of the likes of Perdy and me how anythin' gets done when it comes to fellas. T'ain't no secret, though, is it? Let's just say we had it all planned: puttin' a spark to this place and takin' over once we saw Tom and y'self gettin' busy. Weren't no sweat for us — sweatin' more on yuh takin' out them raiders. Some shootin' there, mister.'

'Don't wanna go makin' a habit of it,' said Ed. 'All too much for a peaceable lawman.'

'Well, that peaceable lawman had best get to figurin' what we gonna do with this dirt-scratchin' bunch. This piece here is gettin' heavy!'

'Turn 'em loose,' shrugged Ed. 'Unless, o' course, yuh got a personal grudge against 'em.'

'Hell, no, they got themselves in the mess. Damn fools — but don't go kiddin' y'self any about what they had in mind for young Holly. She's lucky, real lucky. She had a true pa.' Dori grunted. 'Still, I guess yuh right, Sheriff. We turn 'em loose — damn it, they ain't got a deal left, have they?'

'And then get ourselves out best we can. Be a real pleasure to set our noses for Trulso.' Ed paused, his gaze moving between the two women. 'Damnit, there I go assumin' — '

'Perdy and me ain't goin' no place, mister, if that's what yuh thinkin'. So if Trulso's got anythin' remotely resemblin' a tub, hot water, real soap and the chance for a gal to get outa tick-bitin' rags, we're for it! Meantime, what about that fella and his young 'un? Yuh thought about what's to become of them, Sheriff? Where's their future goin' to take root? Figure we all got an interest in that, ain't we?'

★ ★ ★

Folk these days reaching the high plain out of Trulso on the long haul west still

261

hear tell of the lone home-steader left for dead in the flames of some rough raiders' pillage, and of how he came to trail the Broken Necks in search of his kidnapped daughter. Chances are they will have heard the story from townfolk always anxious to set the record straight:

'Sure, the fellow found his daughter, *and* brought her home, and, yep, it's a fact, Sheriff Woods and that pretty young wife of his, Perdy, were right alongside of him; and, sure, the fellow is still out there on the plain; built himself a new place, married again, and him and Dori and Holly are always real pleased to welcome folk passin' through.

'But as for all that talk about Tom Huckerman bein' some big name gunslinger from way back, boastin' fancy twin Colts and shootin' faster than them scumbag Coyne brothers, heck, that really is all talk. Why, Tom ain't never been seen to wear a gun, and even if he had, he's long since hung it